O9-AIF-408

epic!

CAT NINJA

TIME HEIST

Written by
Matthew Cody

Illustrated by
Chad Thomas

Colors by
Warren Wucinich

Cat Ninja created by Matthew Cody and Yehudi Mercado

Cat Ninja: Time Heist text and illustrations copyright © 2021 by Epic!
Creations, Inc. All rights reserved. Printed in China. No part of this book may
be used or reproduced in any manner whatsoever without written permission
except in the case of reprints in the context of reviews.

Andrews McMeel Publishing
a division of Andrews McMeel Universal
1130 Walnut Street, Kansas City, Missouri 64106

www.andrewsmcmeel.com

Epic! Creations, Inc.
702 Marshall Street, Suite 280
Redwood City, California 94063

www.getepic.com

21 22 23 24 25 SDB 10 9 8 7 6 5 4 3 2 1

Paperback ISBN: 978-1-5248-6758-4
Hardback ISBN: 978-1-5248-6808-6

Library of Congress Control Number: 2021934839

Design by Dan Nordskog

Made by:
King Yip (Dongguan) Printing & Packaging Factory Ltd.
Address and location of manufacturer:
Daning Administrative District, Humen Town
Dongguan Guangdong, China 523930
1st Printing — 7/5/21

ATTENTION: SCHOOLS AND BUSINESSES
Andrews McMeel books are available at quantity discounts with
bulk purchase for educational, business, or sales promotional use.
For information, please e-mail the Andrews McMeel Publishing
Special Sales Department: specialsales@amuniversal.com.

To Master Hamster—the hero we need
—MC

For Jil—thanks for all your support,
encouragement, and that amazing pair
of pants you got me that one time
—CT

Chapter 1: Fish of Legend

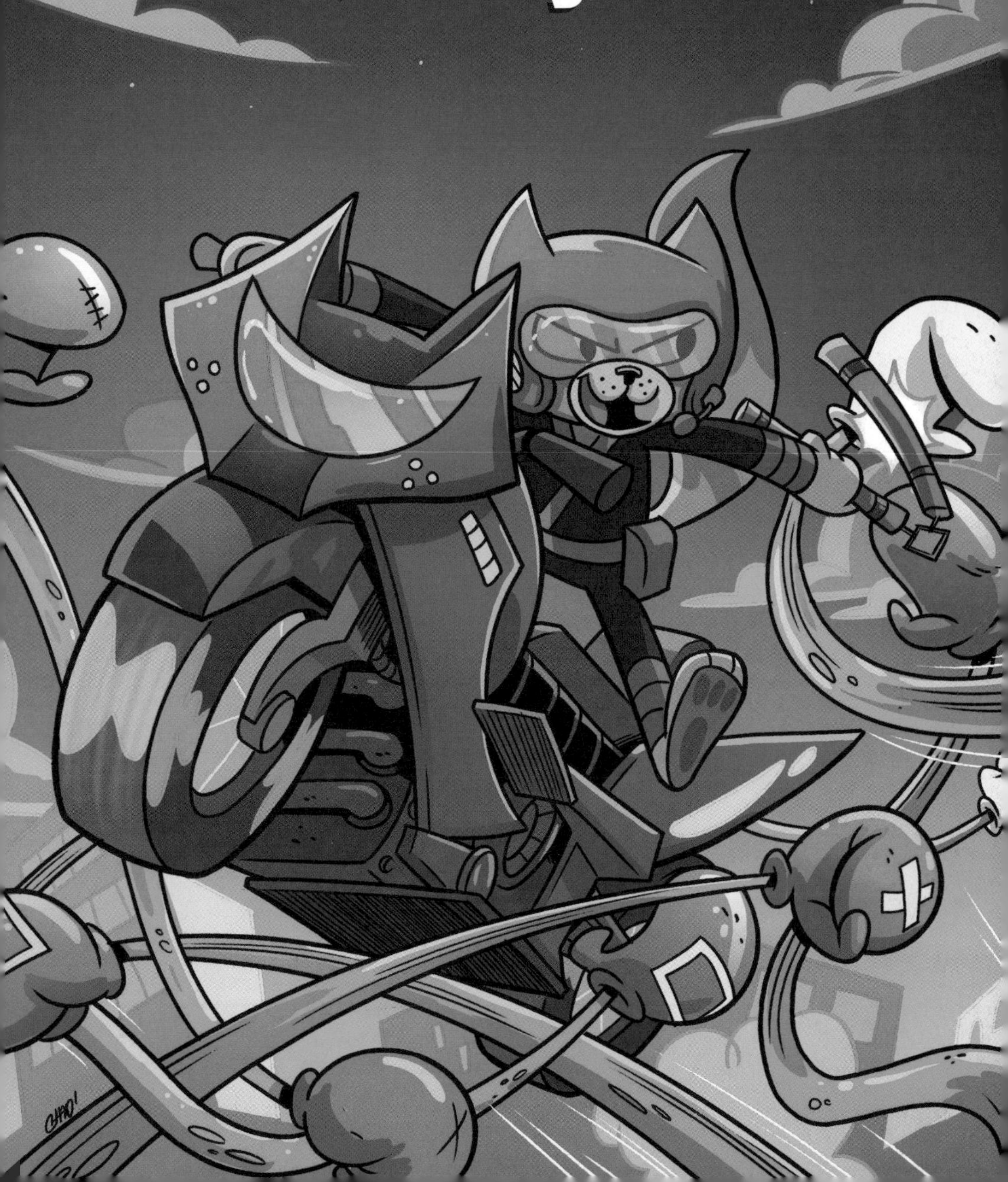

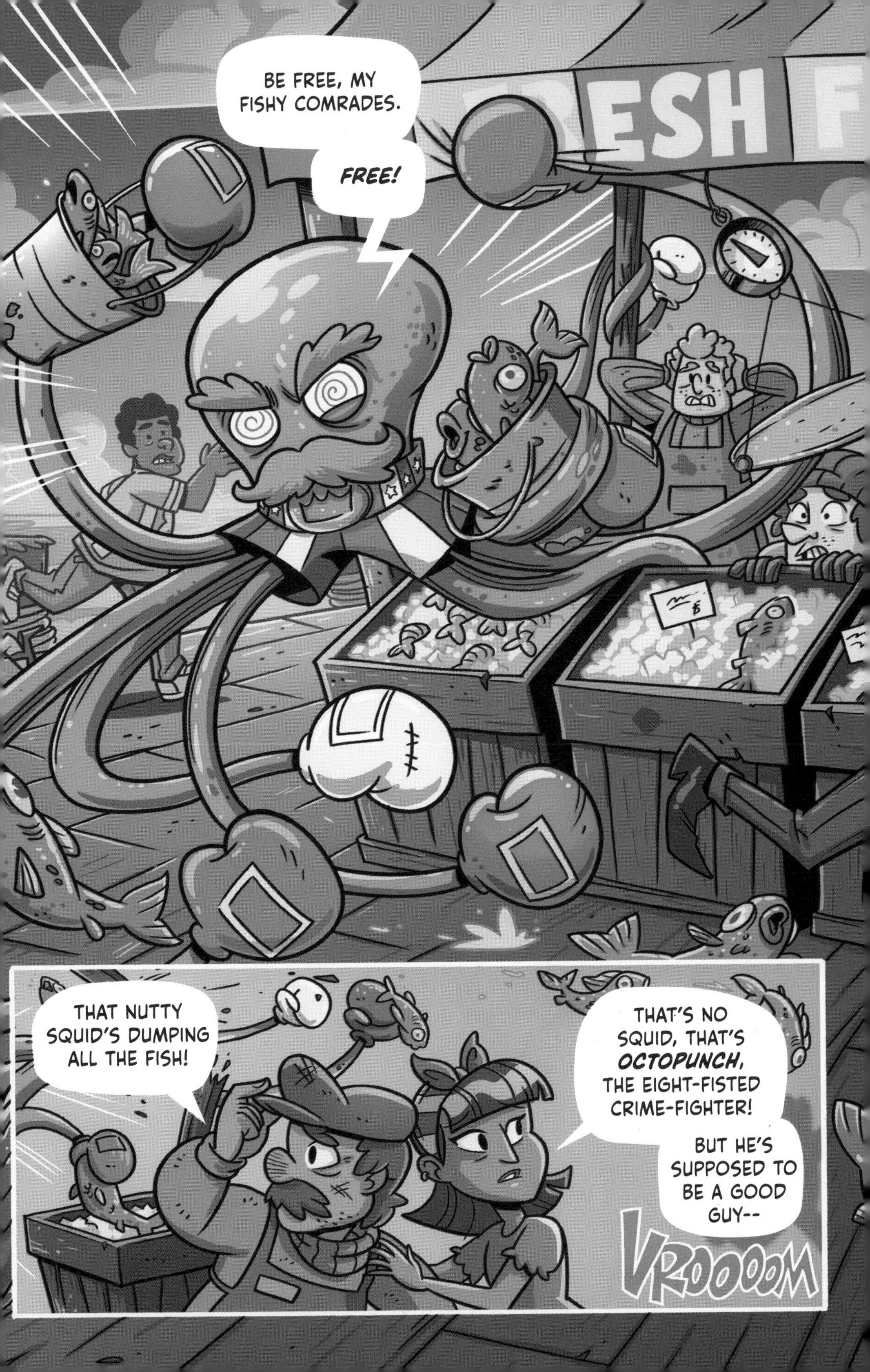
BE FREE, MY FISHY COMRADES.
FREE!
FRESH F
THAT NUTTY SQUID'S DUMPING ALL THE FISH!
THAT'S NO SQUID, THAT'S OCTOPUNCH, THE EIGHT-FISTED CRIME-FIGHTER!
BUT HE'S SUPPOSED TO BE A GOOD GUY--
VROOOOM

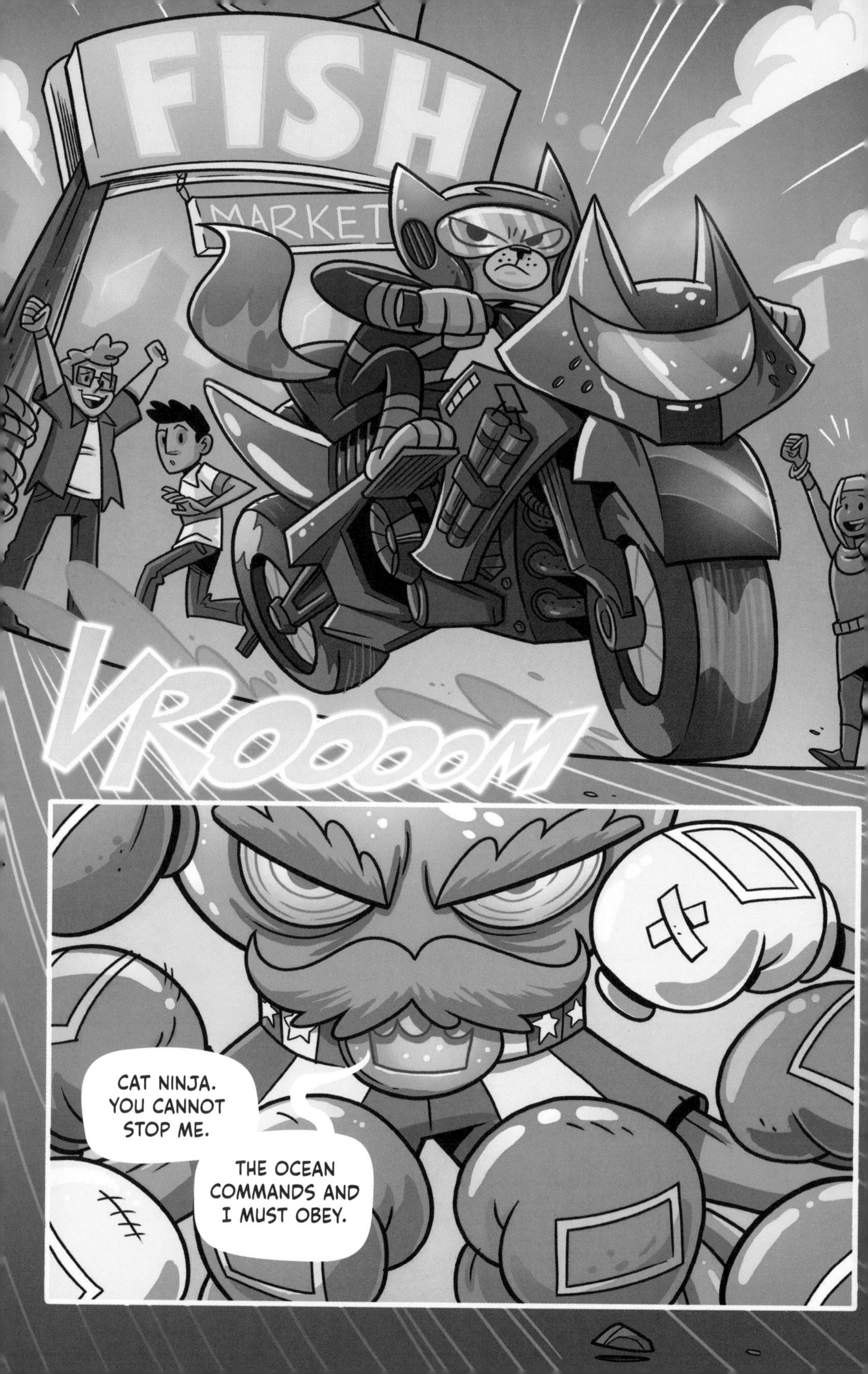
FISH
MARKET
VROOOOM
CAT NINJA. YOU CANNOT STOP ME.
THE OCEAN COMMANDS AND I MUST OBEY.

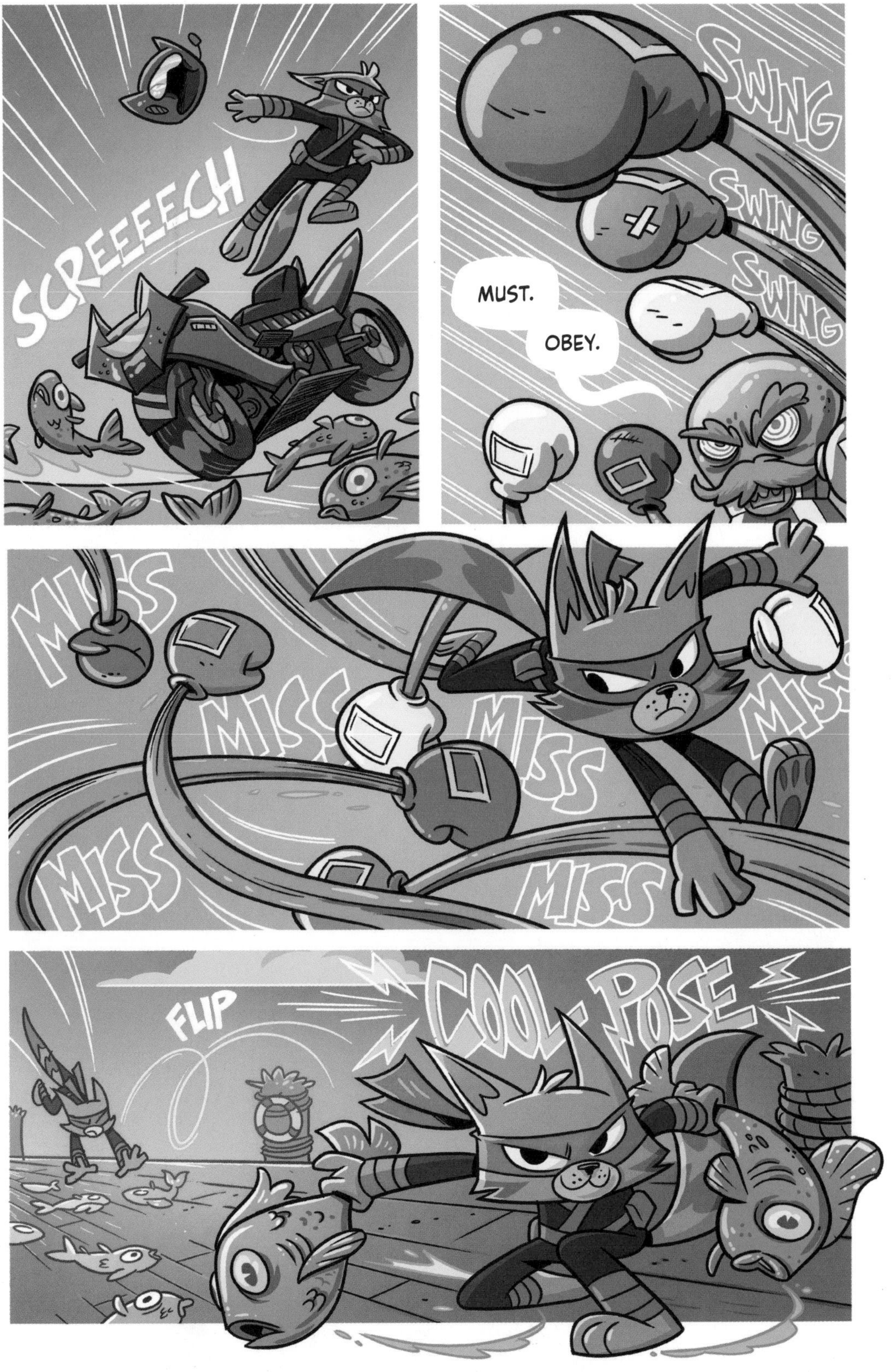
SCREEEEECH
SWING
SWING
SWING
MUST.
OBEY.
MISS
MISS
MISS
MISS
MISS
MISS
FLIP
COOL POSE

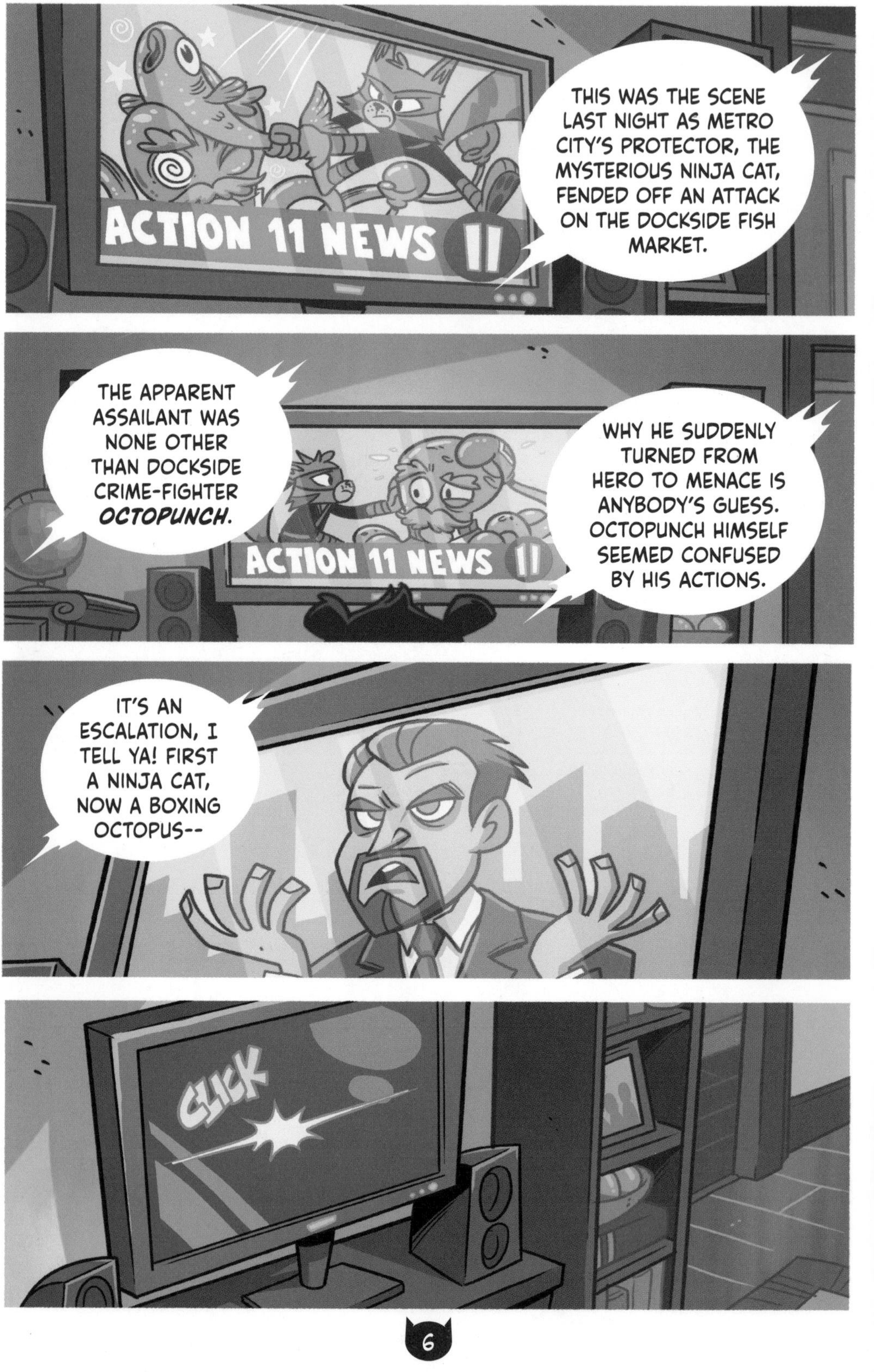
ACTION 11 NEWS
THIS WAS THE SCENE LAST NIGHT AS METRO CITY'S PROTECTOR, THE MYSTERIOUS NINJA CAT, FENDED OFF AN ATTACK ON THE DOCKSIDE FISH MARKET.
THE APPARENT ASSAILANT WAS NONE OTHER THAN DOCKSIDE CRIME-FIGHTER *OCTOPUNCH*.
ACTION 11 NEWS
WHY HE SUDDENLY TURNED FROM HERO TO MENACE IS ANYBODY'S GUESS. OCTOPUNCH HIMSELF SEEMED CONFUSED BY HIS ACTIONS.
IT'S AN ESCALATION, I TELL YA! FIRST A NINJA CAT, NOW A BOXING OCTOPUS--
CLICK

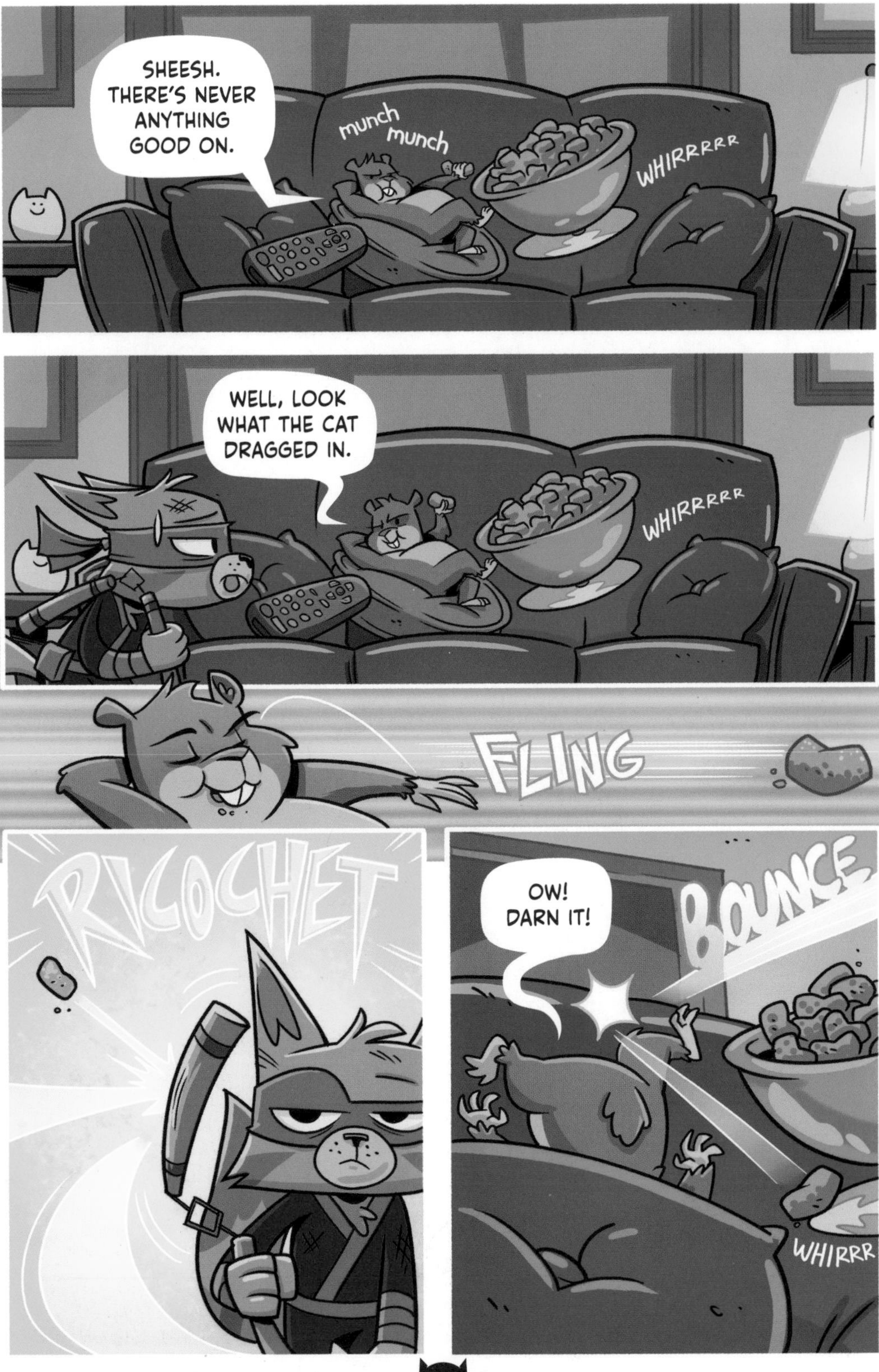
SHEESH. THERE'S NEVER ANYTHING GOOD ON.
munch munch
WHIRRRRR
WELL, LOOK WHAT THE CAT DRAGGED IN.
WHIRRRRR
FLING
RICOCHET
OW! DARN IT!
BOUNCE
WHIRRR

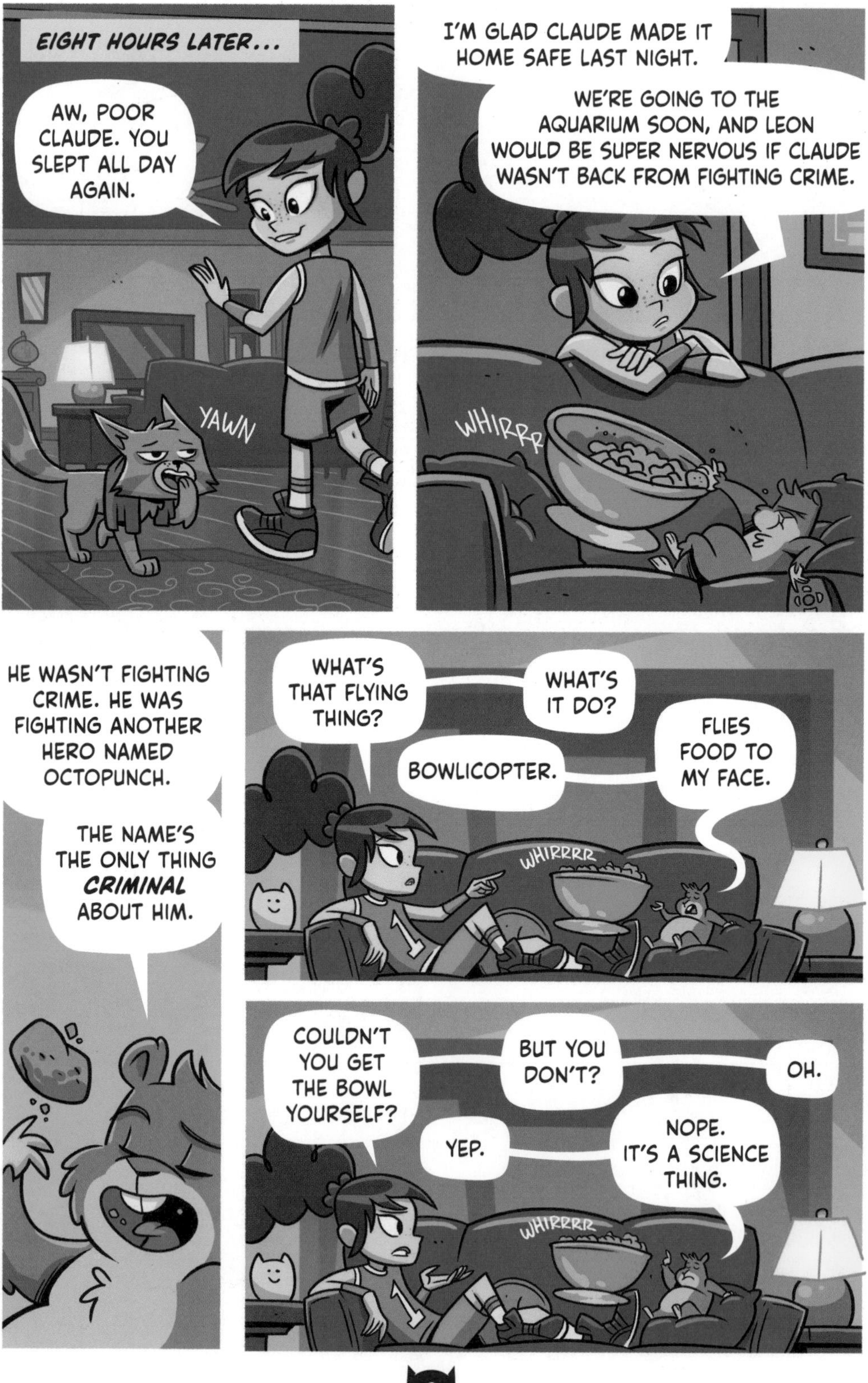
EIGHT HOURS LATER...
AW, POOR CLAUDE. YOU SLEPT ALL DAY AGAIN.
YAWN
I'M GLAD CLAUDE MADE IT HOME SAFE LAST NIGHT.
WE'RE GOING TO THE AQUARIUM SOON, AND LEON WOULD BE SUPER NERVOUS IF CLAUDE WASN'T BACK FROM FIGHTING CRIME.
WHIRRR
HE WASN'T FIGHTING CRIME. HE WAS FIGHTING ANOTHER HERO NAMED OCTOPUNCH.
THE NAME'S THE ONLY THING CRIMINAL ABOUT HIM.
WHAT'S THAT FLYING THING?
BOWLICOPTER.
WHAT'S IT DO?
FLIES FOOD TO MY FACE.
WHIRRRR
COULDN'T YOU GET THE BOWL YOURSELF?
YEP.
BUT YOU DON'T?
NOPE. IT'S A SCIENCE THING.
OH.
WHIRRRR

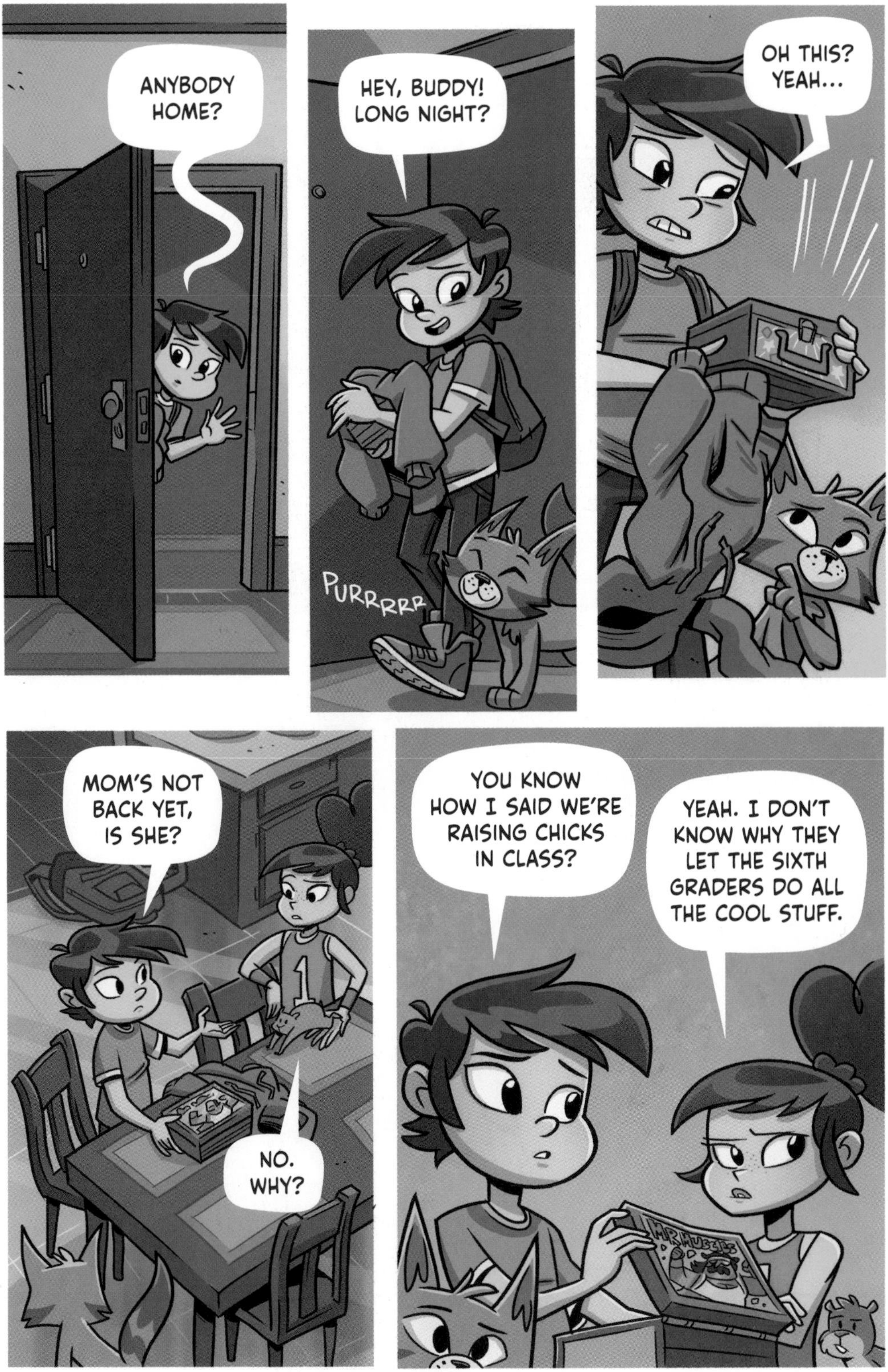
ANYBODY HOME?
HEY, BUDDY! LONG NIGHT?
PURRRRRR
OH THIS? YEAH...
MOM'S NOT BACK YET, IS SHE?
NO. WHY?
YOU KNOW HOW I SAID WE'RE RAISING CHICKS IN CLASS?
YEAH. I DON'T KNOW WHY THEY LET THE SIXTH GRADERS DO ALL THE COOL STUFF.

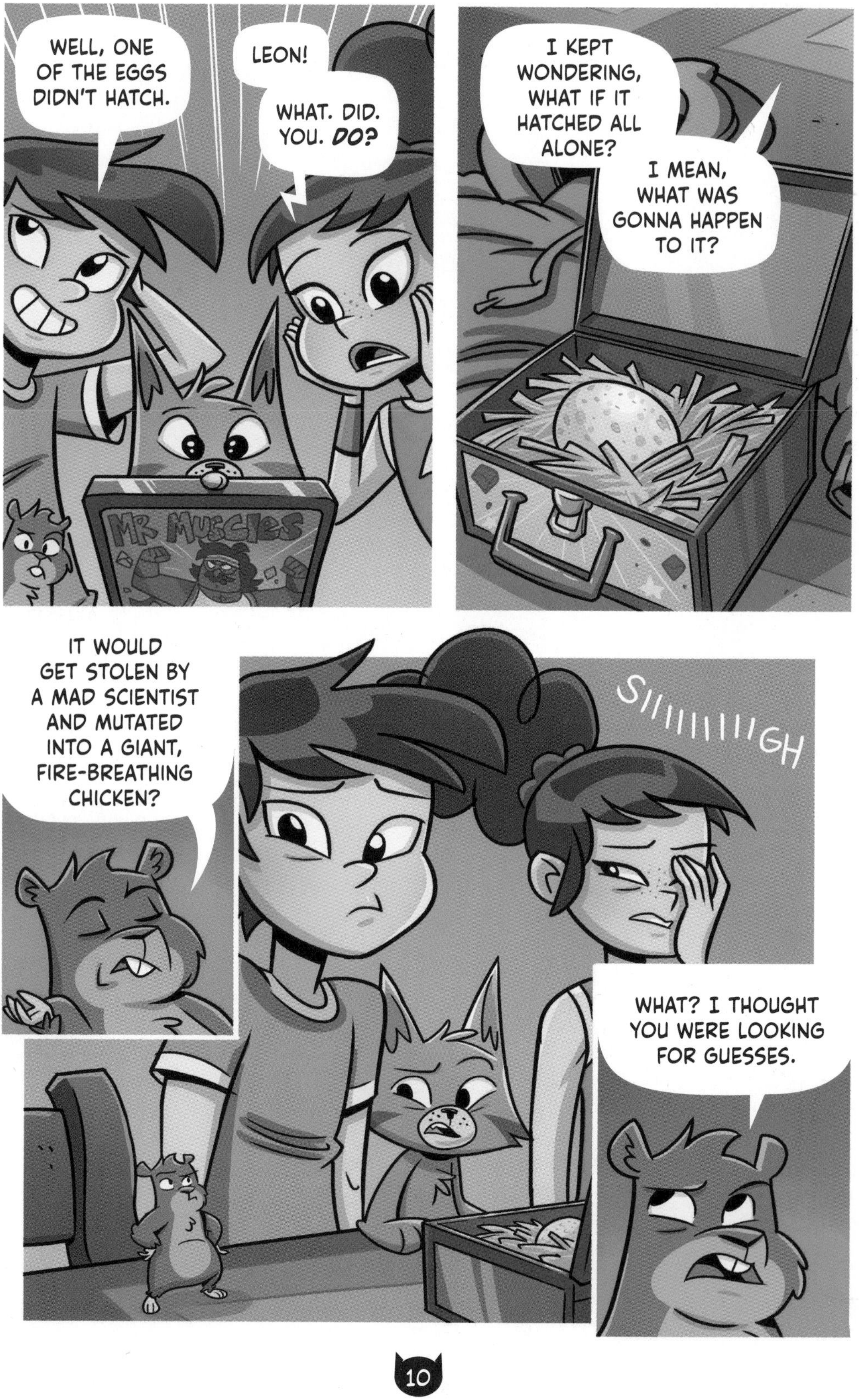
WELL, ONE OF THE EGGS DIDN'T HATCH.
LEON!
WHAT. DID. YOU. *DO?*
MR MUSCLES
I KEPT WONDERING, WHAT IF IT HATCHED ALL ALONE?
I MEAN, WHAT WAS GONNA HAPPEN TO IT?
IT WOULD GET STOLEN BY A MAD SCIENTIST AND MUTATED INTO A GIANT, FIRE-BREATHING CHICKEN?
SIIIIIIIIGH
WHAT? I THOUGHT YOU WERE LOOKING FOR GUESSES.

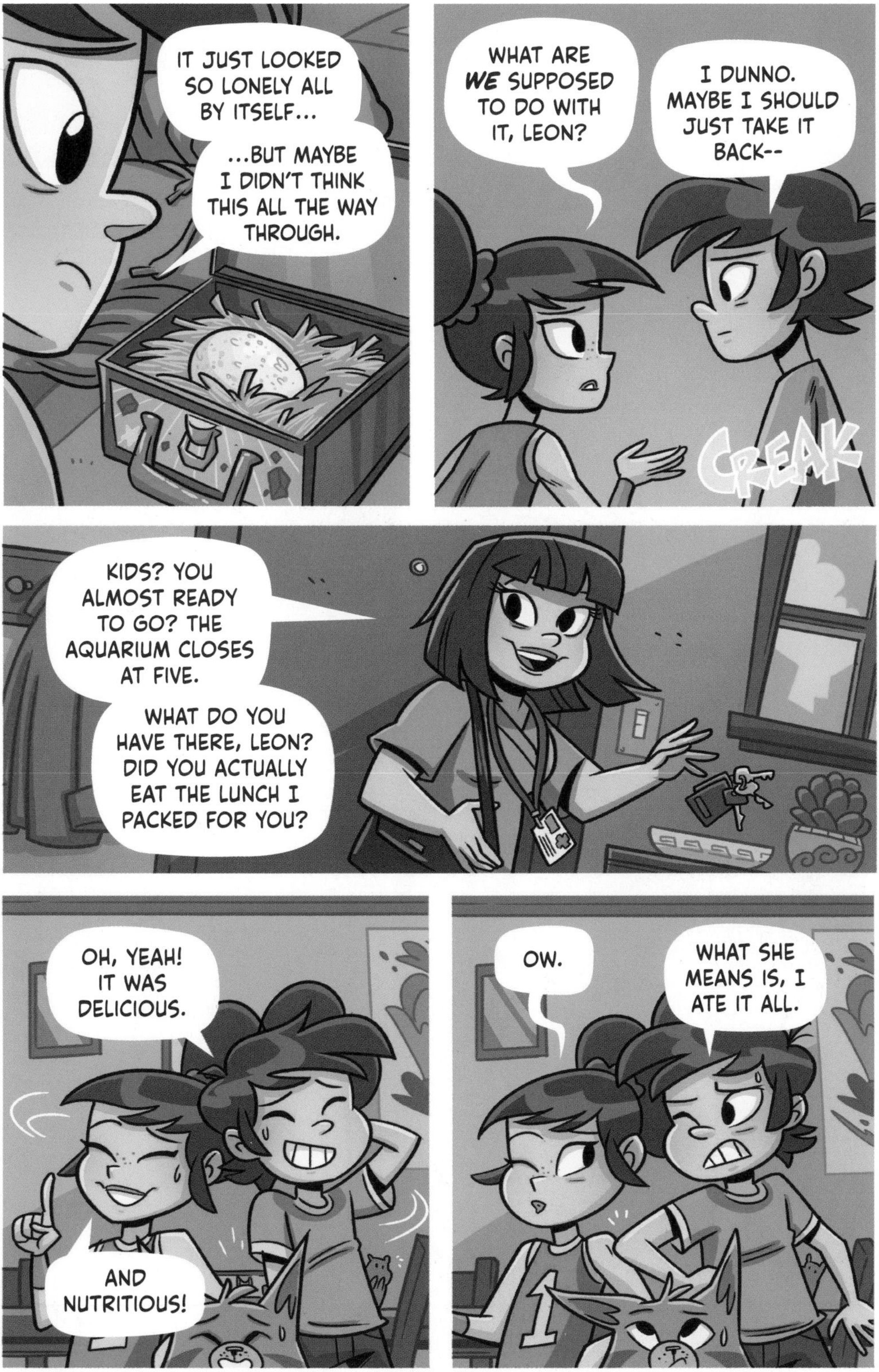
IT JUST LOOKED SO LONELY ALL BY ITSELF...
...BUT MAYBE I DIDN'T THINK THIS ALL THE WAY THROUGH.
WHAT ARE WE SUPPOSED TO DO WITH IT, LEON?
I DUNNO. MAYBE I SHOULD JUST TAKE IT BACK--
CREAK
KIDS? YOU ALMOST READY TO GO? THE AQUARIUM CLOSES AT FIVE.
WHAT DO YOU HAVE THERE, LEON? DID YOU ACTUALLY EAT THE LUNCH I PACKED FOR YOU?
OH, YEAH! IT WAS DELICIOUS.
AND NUTRITIOUS!
OW.
WHAT SHE MEANS IS, I ATE IT ALL.

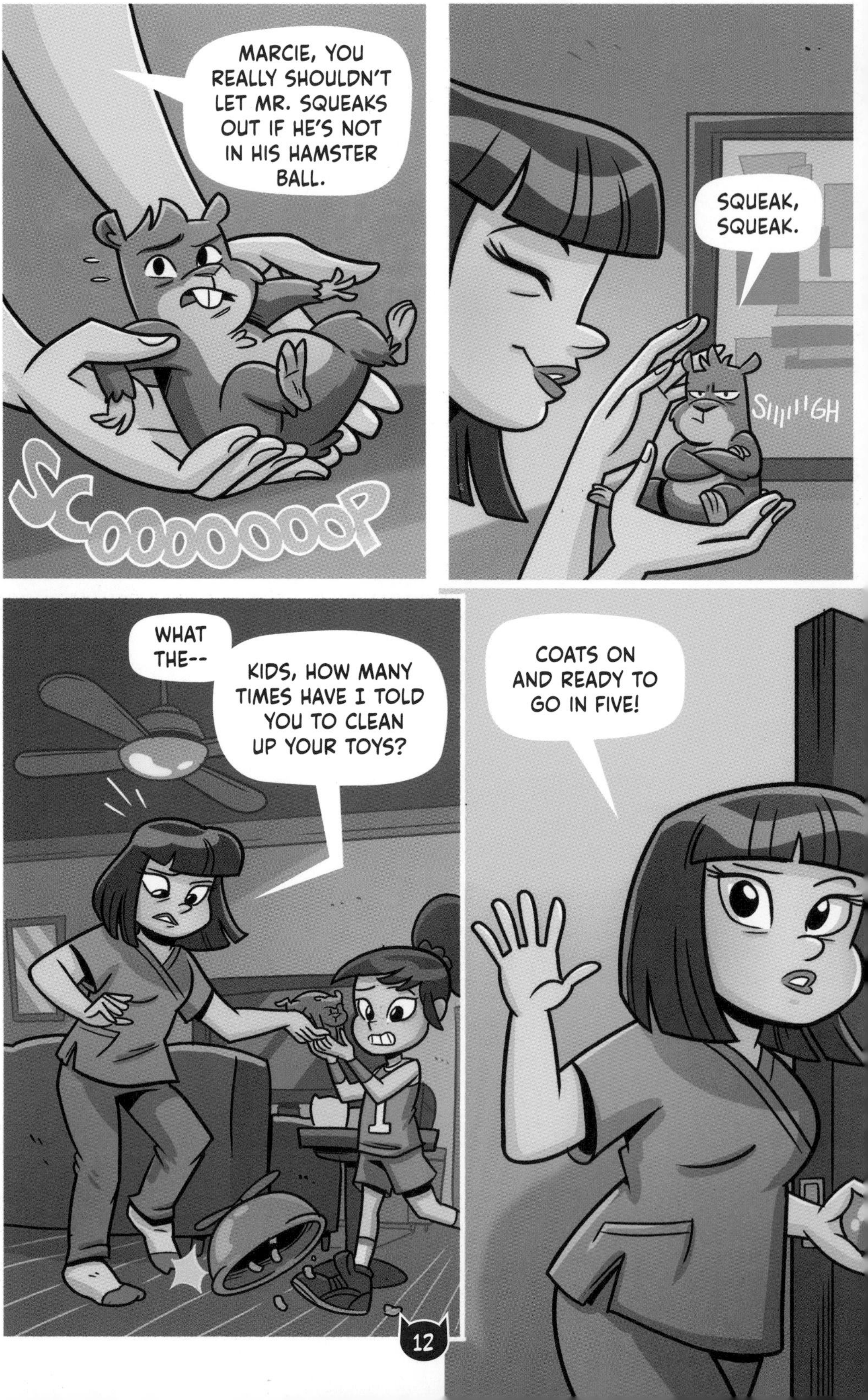
MARCIE, YOU REALLY SHOULDN'T LET MR. SQUEAKS OUT IF HE'S NOT IN HIS HAMSTER BALL.
SCOOOOOOOOP
SQUEAK, SQUEAK.
SIIII''GH
WHAT THE--
KIDS, HOW MANY TIMES HAVE I TOLD YOU TO CLEAN UP YOUR TOYS?
COATS ON AND READY TO GO IN FIVE!

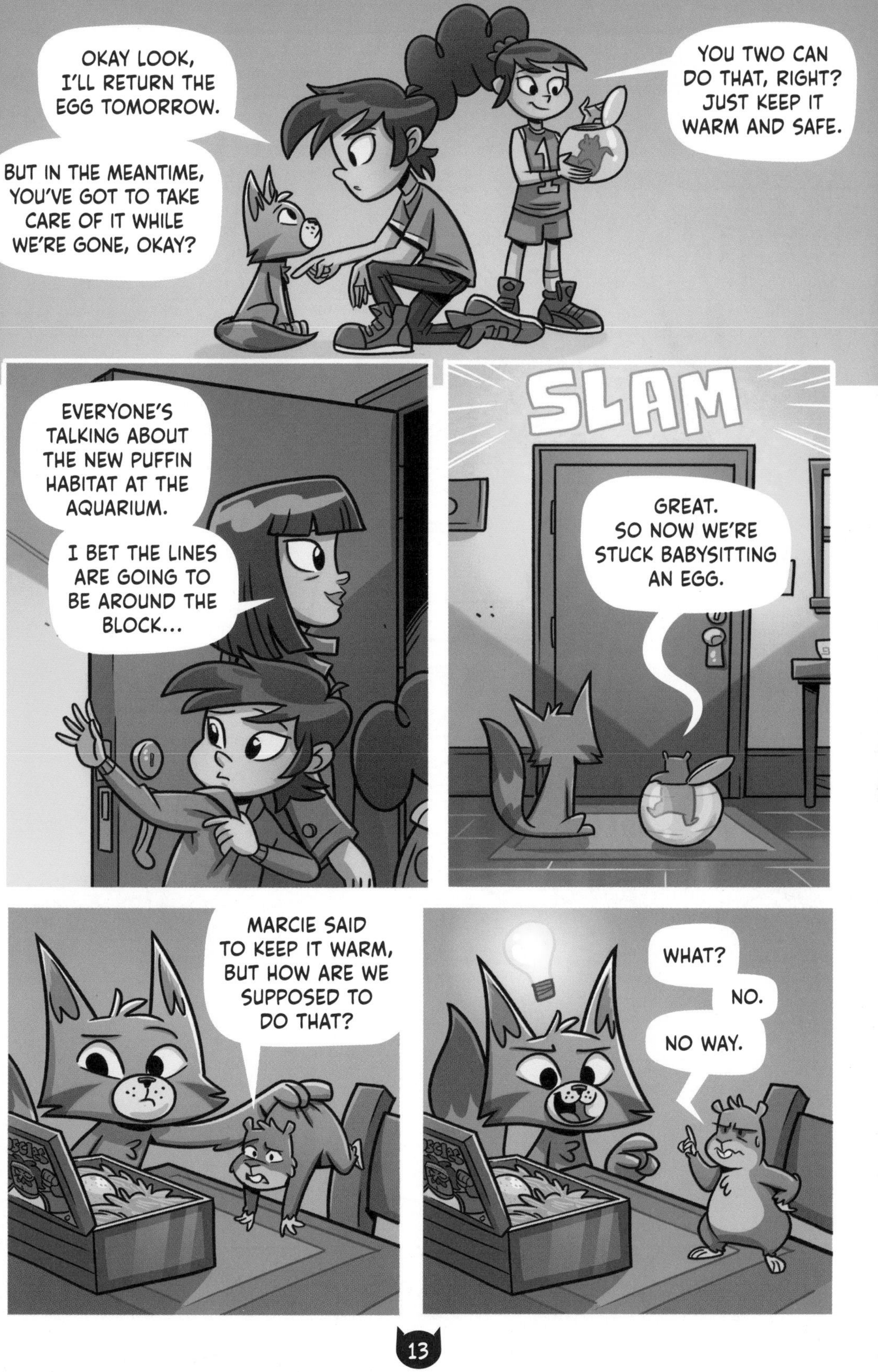

OKAY LOOK, I'LL RETURN THE EGG TOMORROW.
BUT IN THE MEANTIME, YOU'VE GOT TO TAKE CARE OF IT WHILE WE'RE GONE, OKAY?
YOU TWO CAN DO THAT, RIGHT? JUST KEEP IT WARM AND SAFE.
EVERYONE'S TALKING ABOUT THE NEW PUFFIN HABITAT AT THE AQUARIUM.
I BET THE LINES ARE GOING TO BE AROUND THE BLOCK...
SLAM
GREAT. SO NOW WE'RE STUCK BABYSITTING AN EGG.
MARCIE SAID TO KEEP IT WARM, BUT HOW ARE WE SUPPOSED TO DO THAT?
WHAT?
NO.
NO WAY.

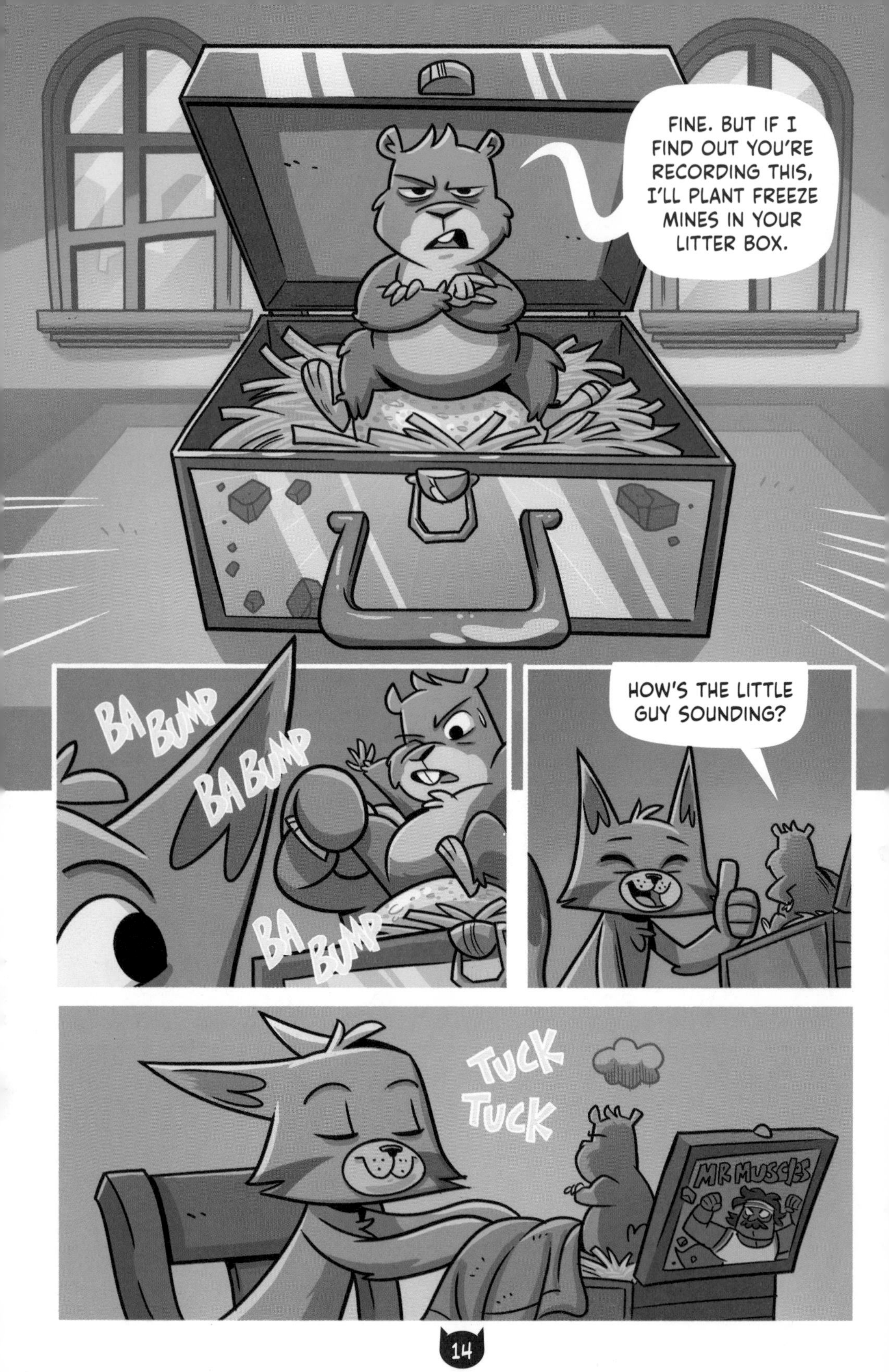
FINE. BUT IF I FIND OUT YOU'RE RECORDING THIS, I'LL PLANT FREEZE MINES IN YOUR LITTER BOX.
BA BUMP
BA BUMP
BA BUMP
HOW'S THE LITTLE GUY SOUNDING?
TUCK TUCK
MR MUSCLES

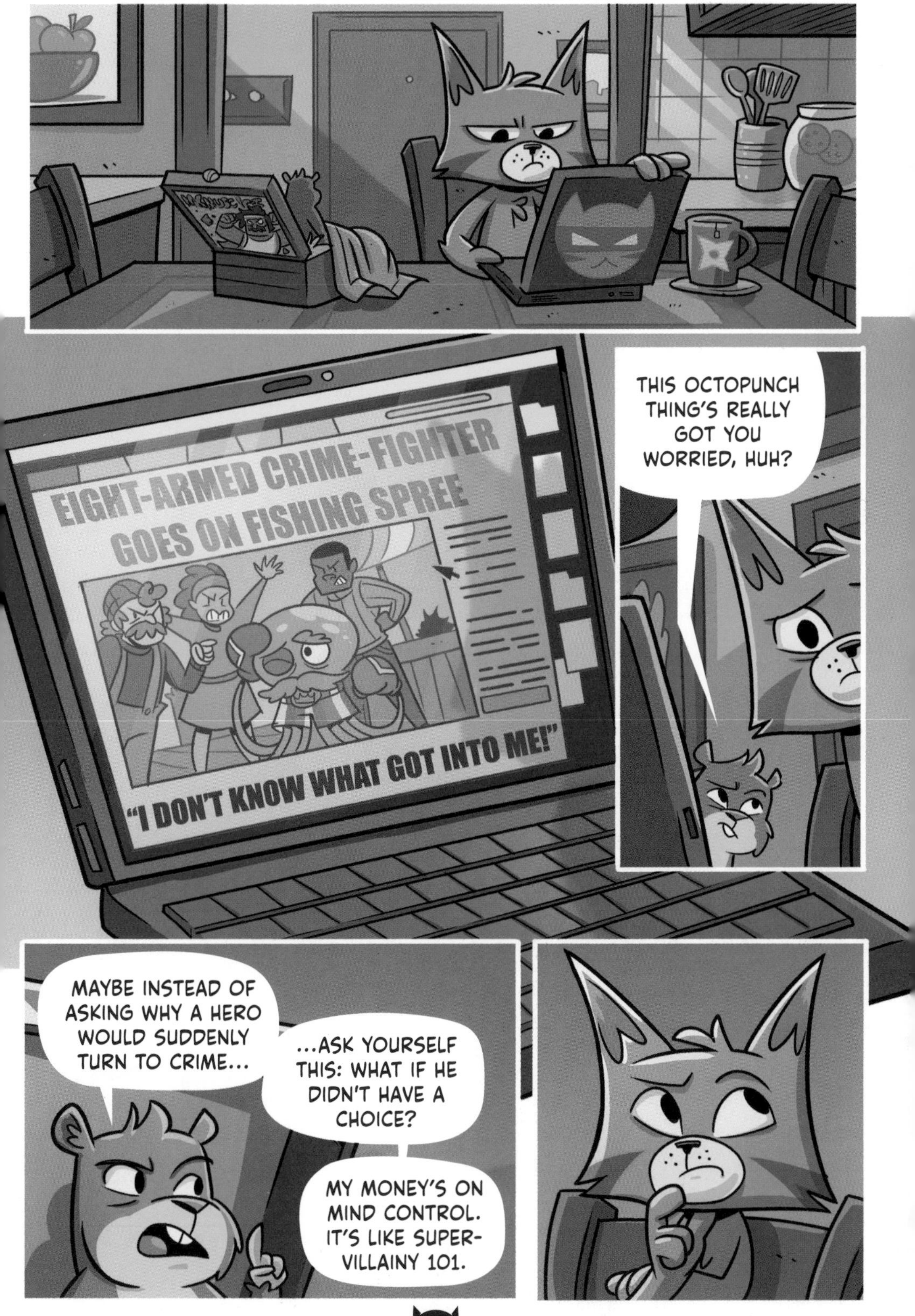
EIGHT-ARMED CRIME-FIGHTER GOES ON FISHING SPREE
"I DON'T KNOW WHAT GOT INTO ME!"
THIS OCTOPUNCH THING'S REALLY GOT YOU WORRIED, HUH?
MAYBE INSTEAD OF ASKING WHY A HERO WOULD SUDDENLY TURN TO CRIME...
...ASK YOURSELF THIS: WHAT IF HE DIDN'T HAVE A CHOICE?
MY MONEY'S ON MIND CONTROL. IT'S LIKE SUPER-VILLAINY 101.

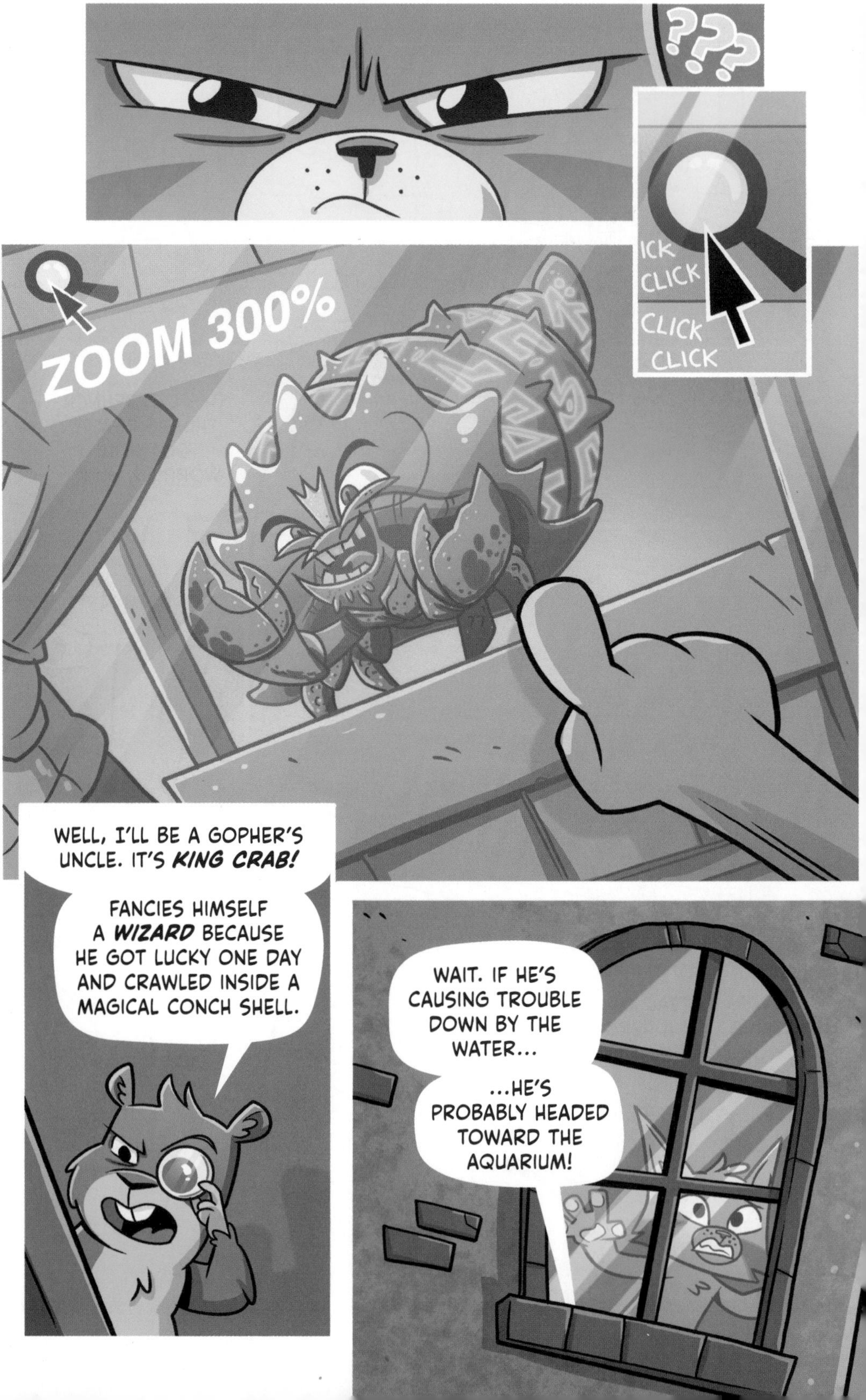
???
ICK
CLICK
CLICK
CLICK
ZOOM 300%
WELL, I'LL BE A GOPHER'S UNCLE. IT'S ***KING CRAB!***
FANCIES HIMSELF A ***WIZARD*** BECAUSE HE GOT LUCKY ONE DAY AND CRAWLED INSIDE A MAGICAL CONCH SHELL.
WAIT. IF HE'S CAUSING TROUBLE DOWN BY THE WATER...
...HE'S PROBABLY HEADED TOWARD THE AQUARIUM!

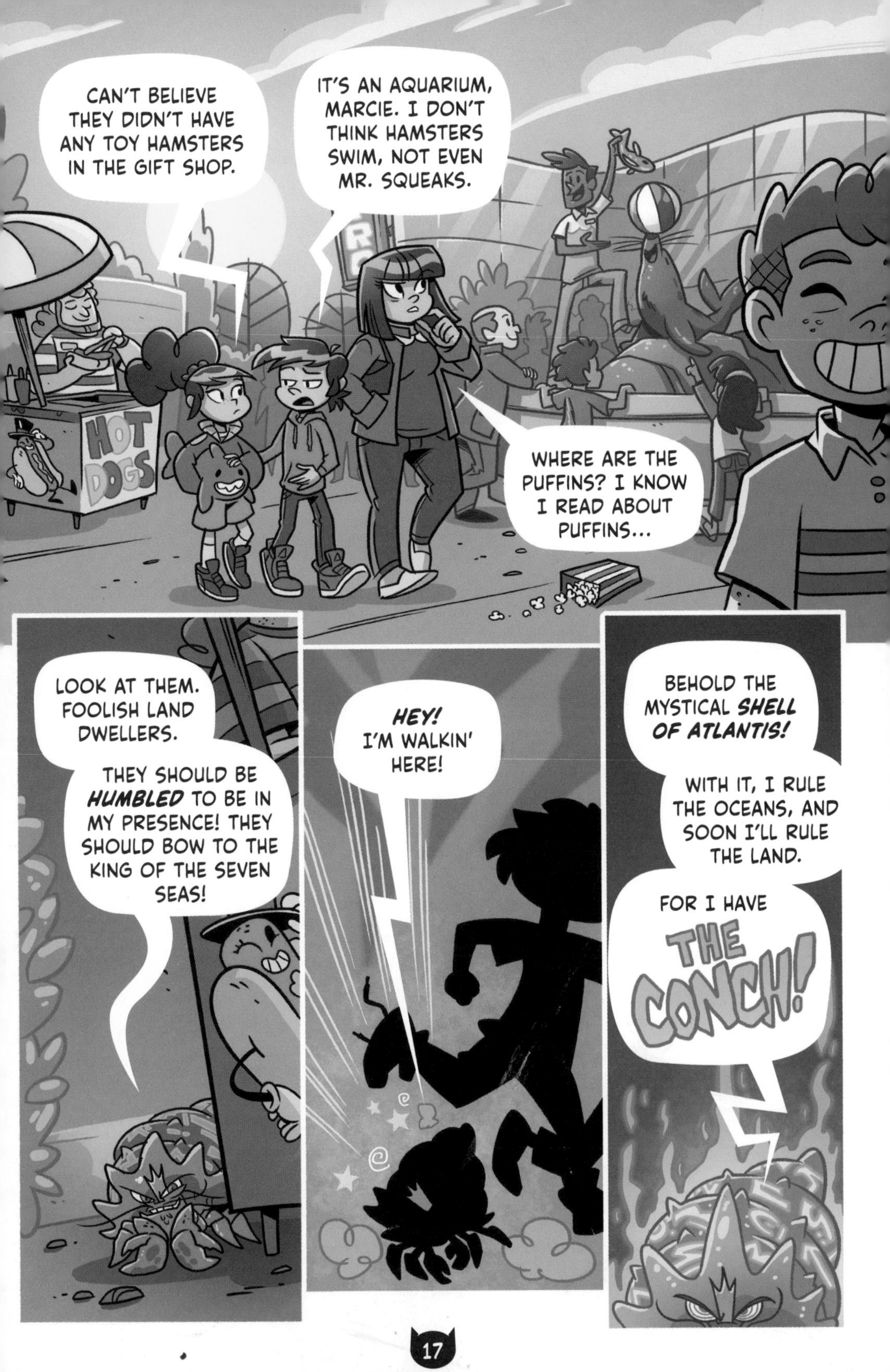
CAN'T BELIEVE THEY DIDN'T HAVE ANY TOY HAMSTERS IN THE GIFT SHOP.
IT'S AN AQUARIUM, MARCIE. I DON'T THINK HAMSTERS SWIM, NOT EVEN MR. SQUEAKS.
WHERE ARE THE PUFFINS? I KNOW I READ ABOUT PUFFINS...
HOT DOGS
LOOK AT THEM. FOOLISH LAND DWELLERS.
THEY SHOULD BE *HUMBLED* TO BE IN MY PRESENCE! THEY SHOULD BOW TO THE KING OF THE SEVEN SEAS!
HEY! I'M WALKIN' HERE!
BEHOLD THE MYSTICAL *SHELL OF ATLANTIS!*
WITH IT, I RULE THE OCEANS, AND SOON I'LL RULE THE LAND.
FOR I HAVE
THE CONCH!

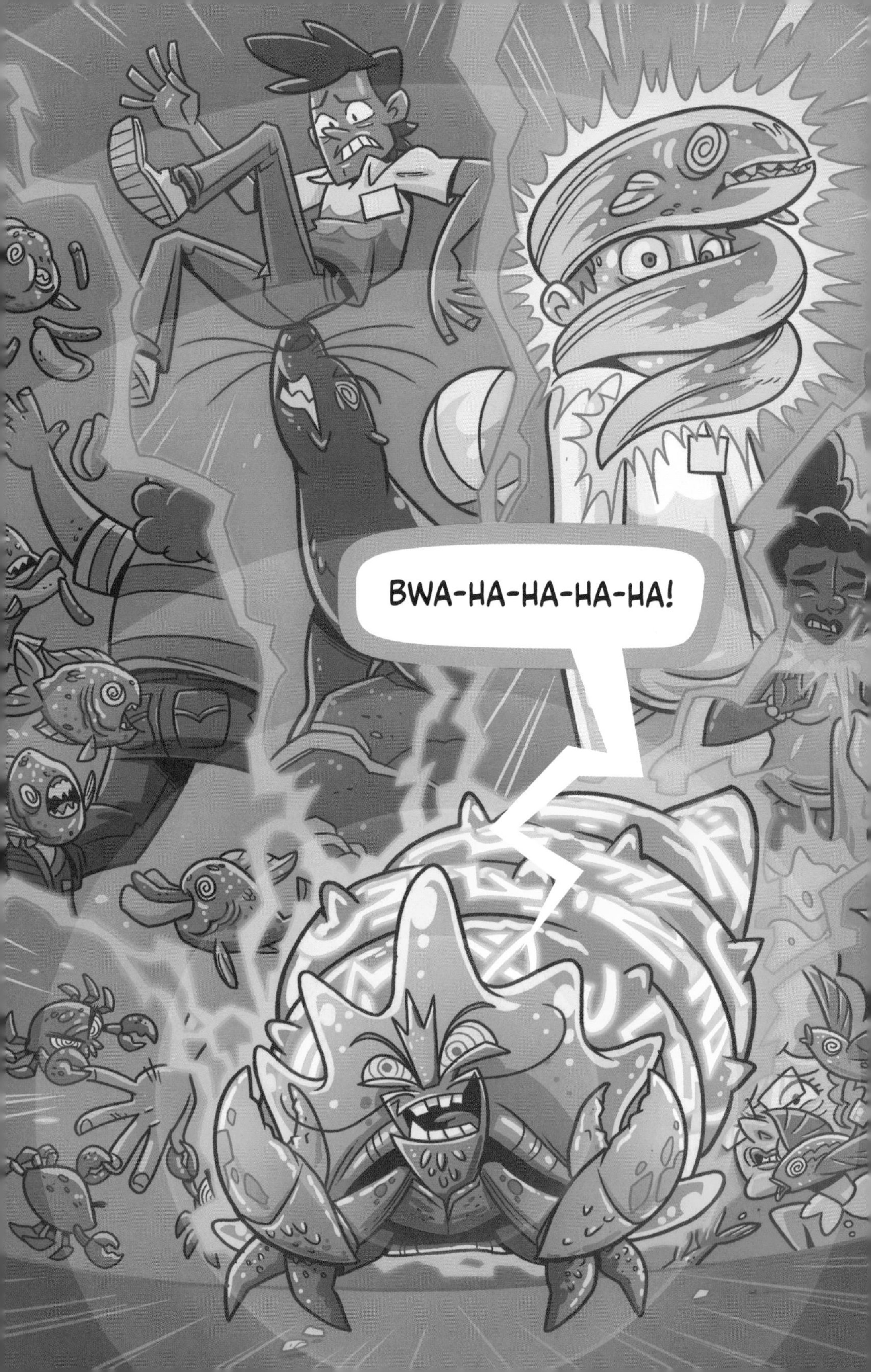
BWA-HA-HA-HA-HA!

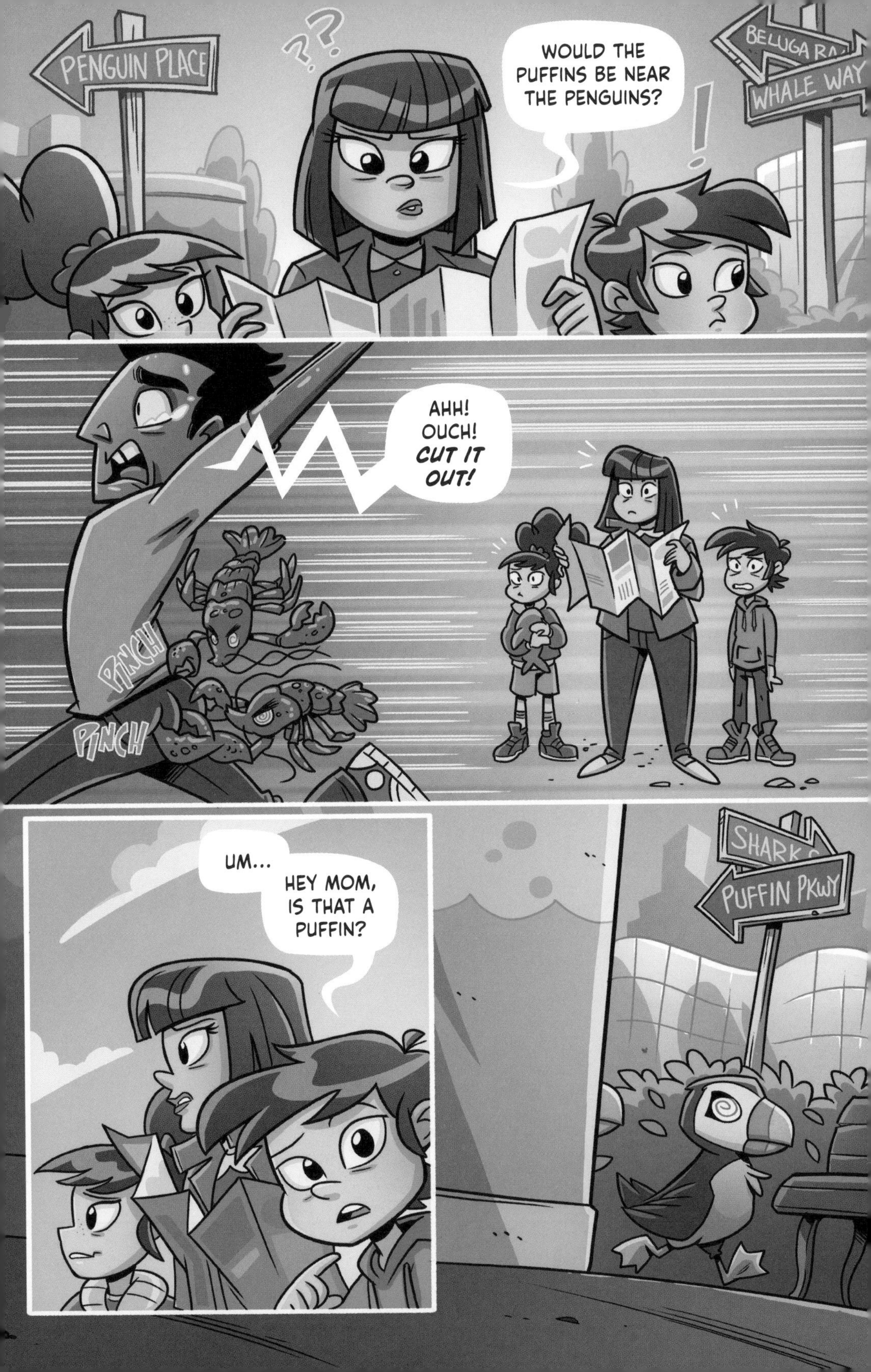
PENGUIN PLACE
BELUGA
WHALE WAY
WOULD THE PUFFINS BE NEAR THE PENGUINS?
AHH! OUCH! *CUT IT OUT!*
PINCH
PINCH
UM...
HEY MOM, IS THAT A PUFFIN?
PUFFIN PKWY

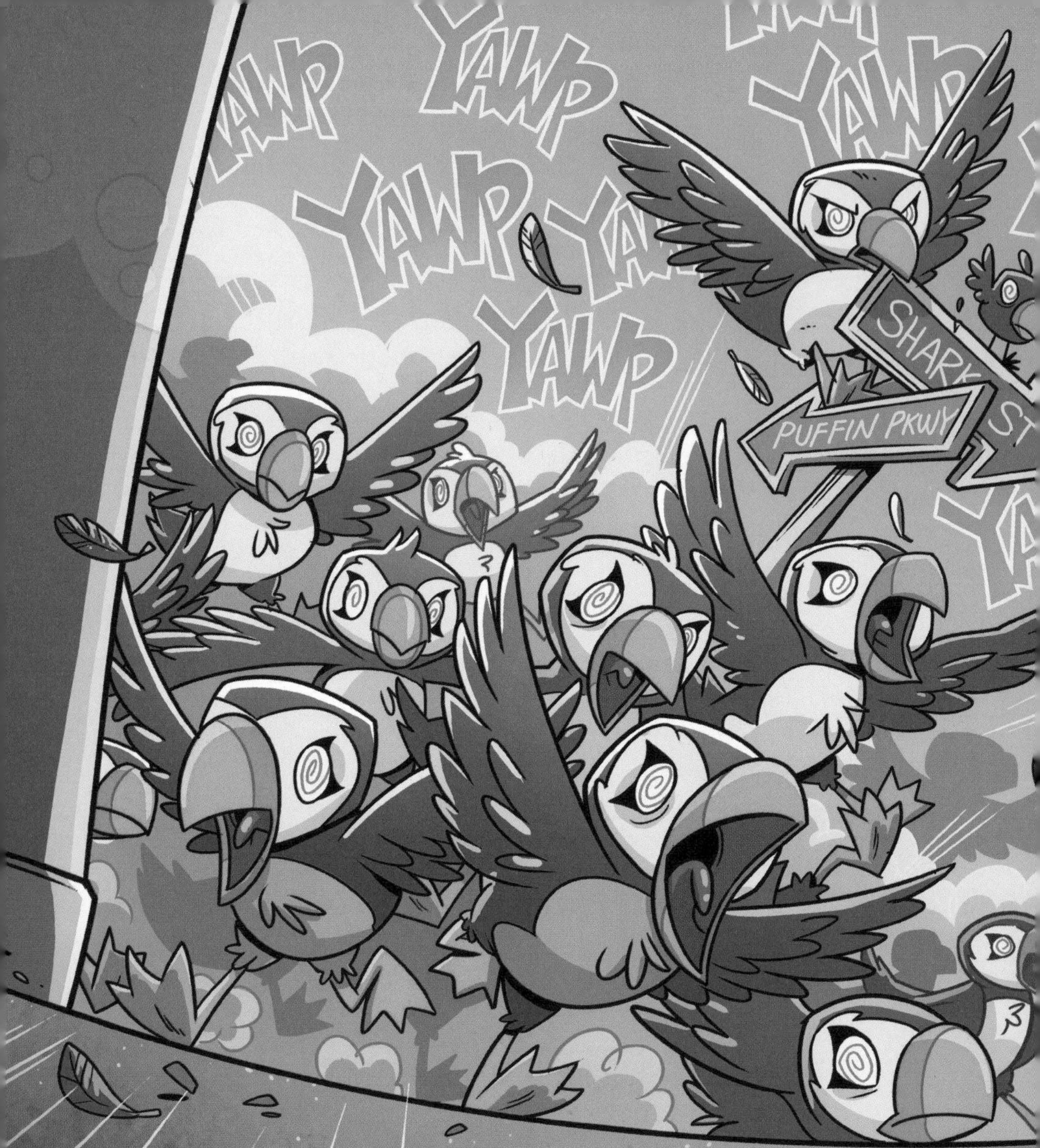
YAWP
YAWP
YAWP
YAWP
YAWP
YAWP
SHARK ST
PUFFIN PKWY

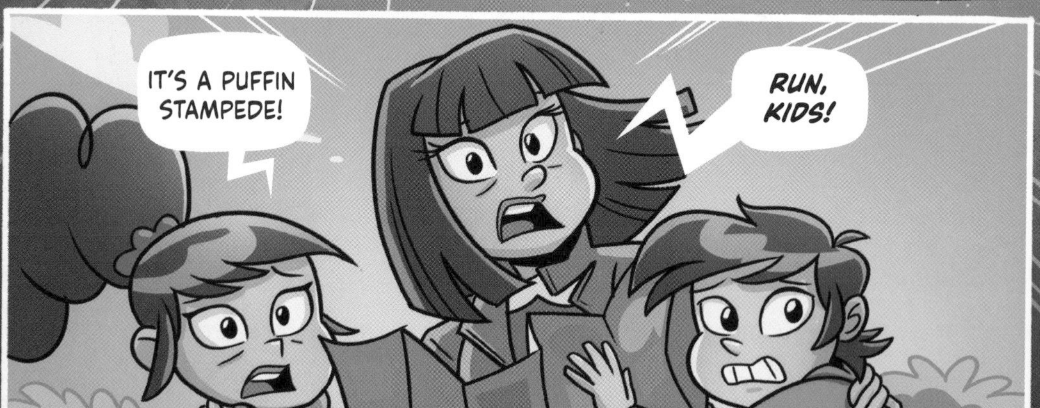
IT'S A PUFFIN STAMPEDE!
RUN, KIDS!

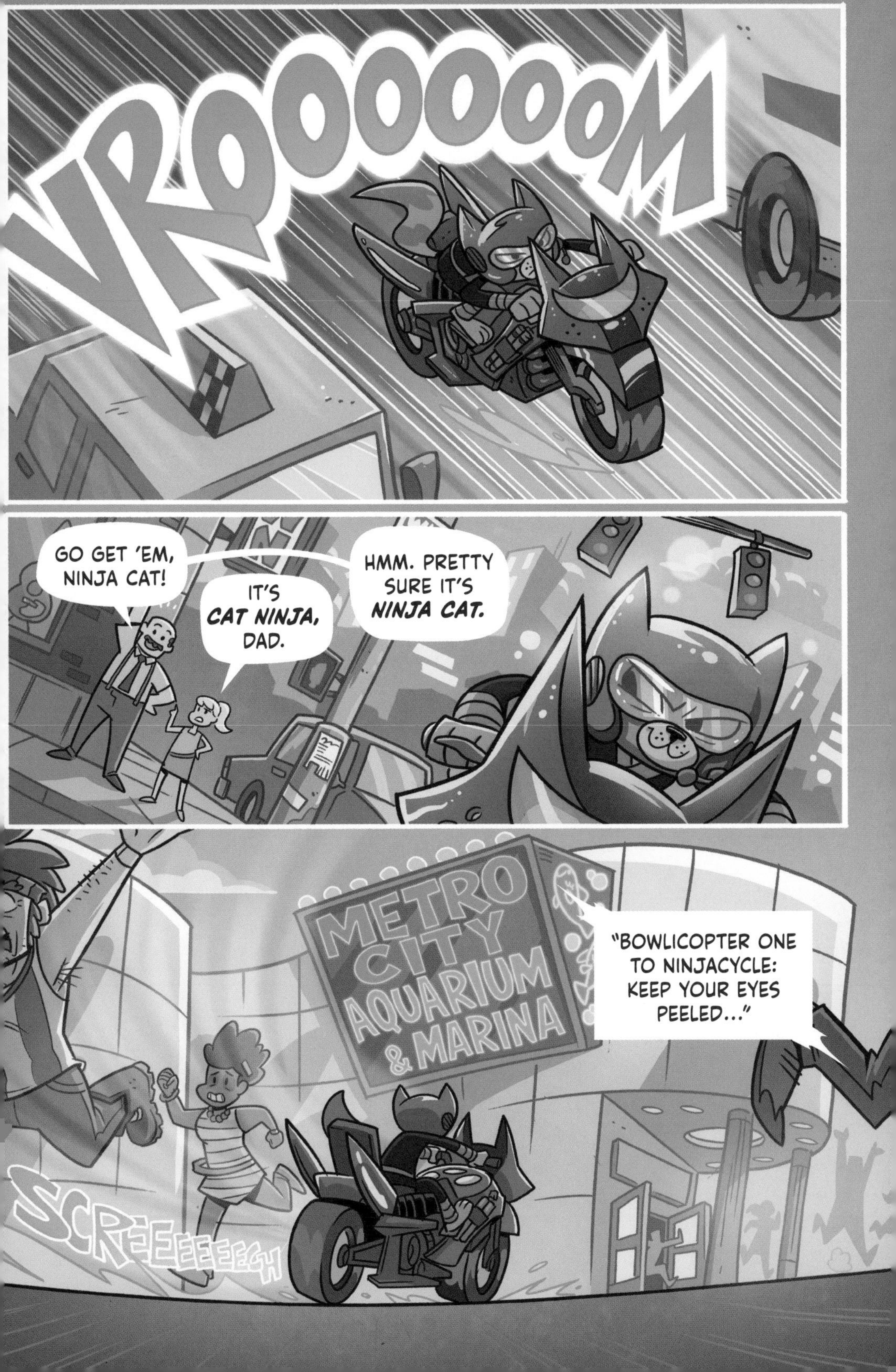
VROOOOOOM
GO GET 'EM, NINJA CAT!
IT'S CAT NINJA, DAD.
HMM. PRETTY SURE IT'S NINJA CAT.
METRO CITY AQUARIUM & MARINA
"BOWLICOPTER ONE TO NINJACYCLE: KEEP YOUR EYES PEELED..."
SCREEEEEEECH

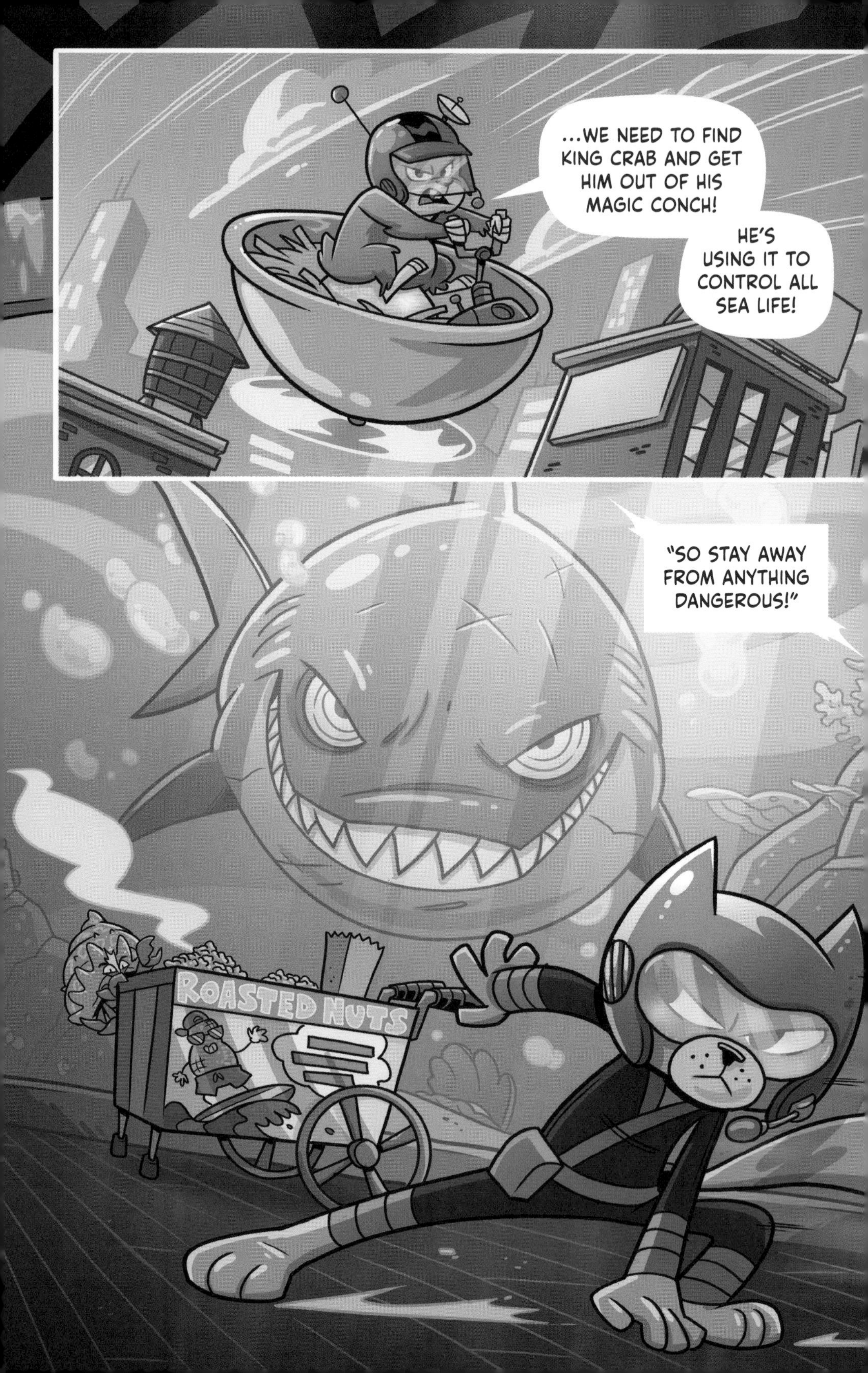
...WE NEED TO FIND KING CRAB AND GET HIM OUT OF HIS MAGIC CONCH!
HE'S USING IT TO CONTROL ALL SEA LIFE!
"SO STAY AWAY FROM ANYTHING DANGEROUS!"
ROASTED NUTS

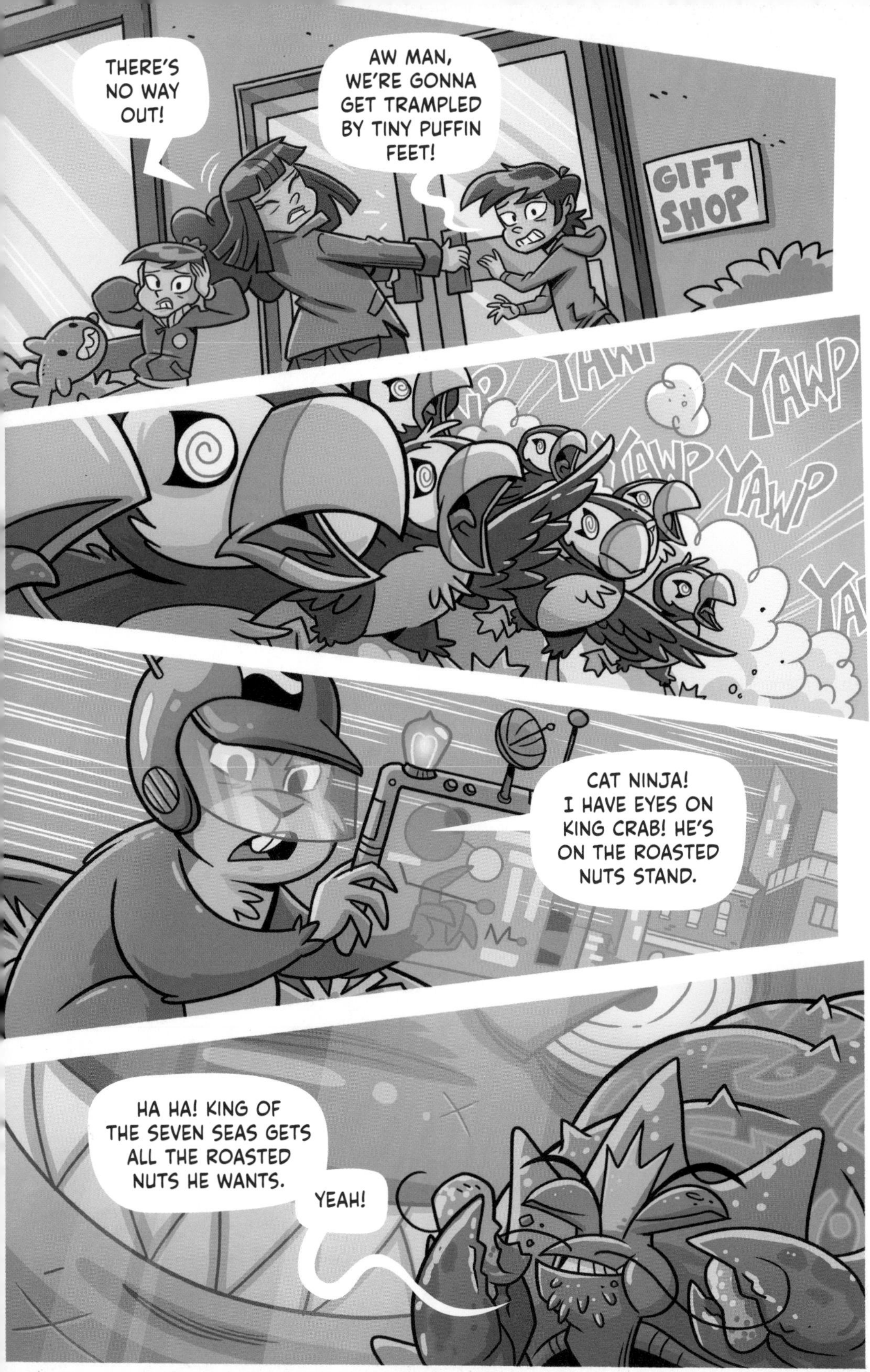
THERE'S NO WAY OUT!
AW MAN, WE'RE GONNA GET TRAMPLED BY TINY PUFFIN FEET!
GIFT SHOP
YAWP
YAWP
YAWP
YAWP
CAT NINJA! I HAVE EYES ON KING CRAB! HE'S ON THE ROASTED NUTS STAND.
HA HA! KING OF THE SEVEN SEAS GETS ALL THE ROASTED NUTS HE WANTS.
YEAH!

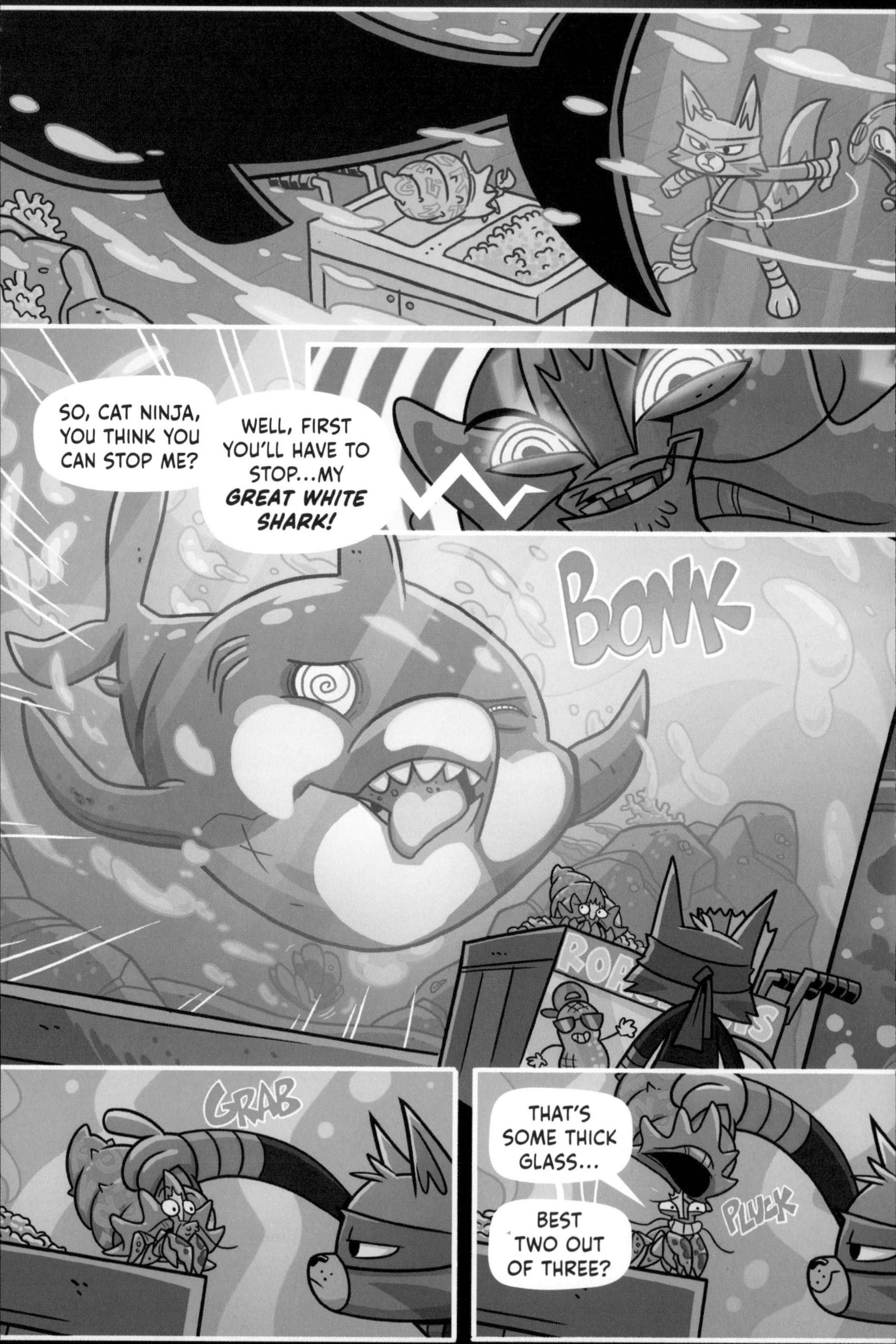
SO, CAT NINJA, YOU THINK YOU CAN STOP ME?
WELL, FIRST YOU'LL HAVE TO STOP...MY *GREAT WHITE SHARK!*
BONK
GRAB
THAT'S SOME THICK GLASS...
PLUCK
BEST TWO OUT OF THREE?

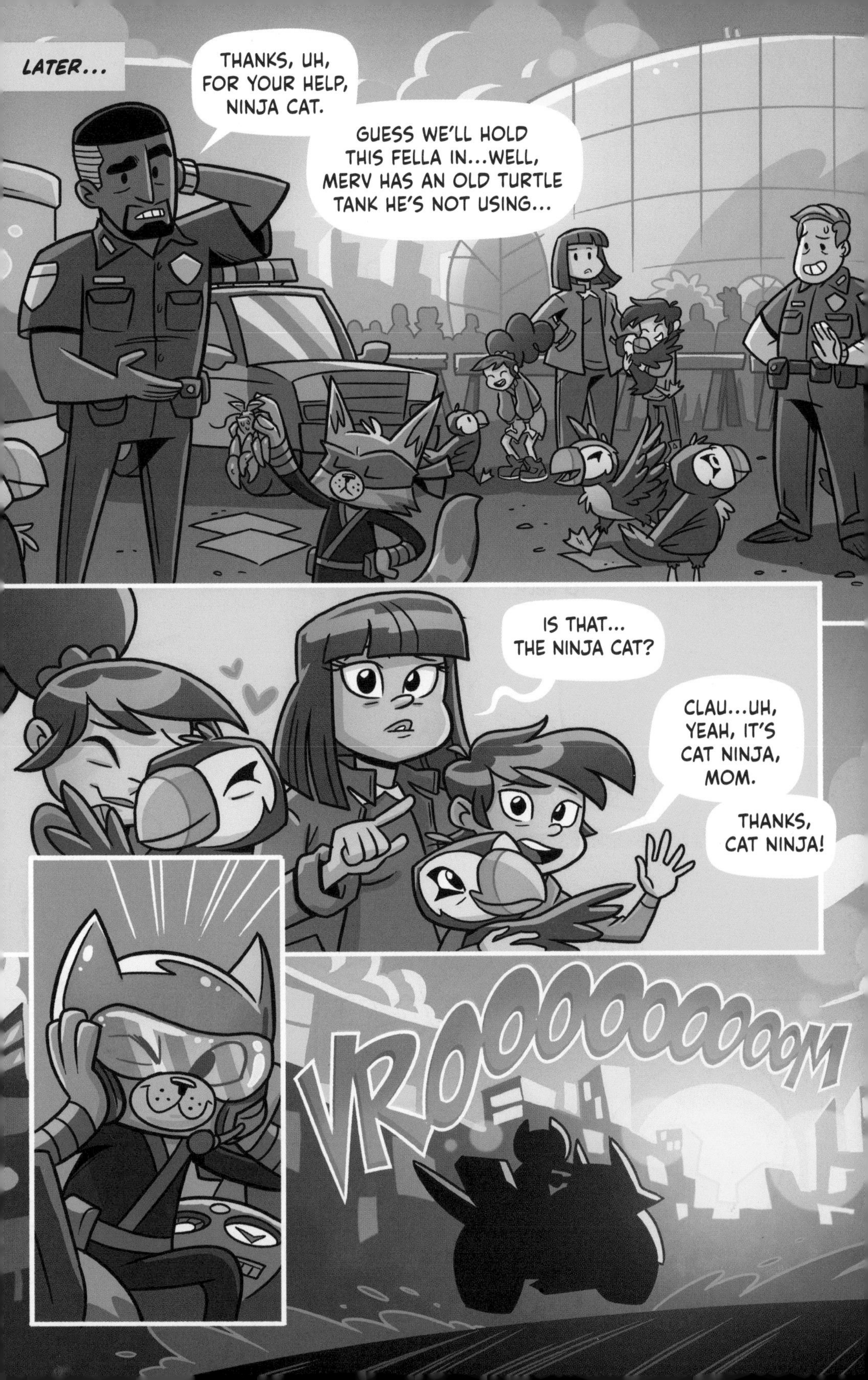
LATER...
THANKS, UH, FOR YOUR HELP, NINJA CAT.
GUESS WE'LL HOLD THIS FELLA IN...WELL, MERV HAS AN OLD TURTLE TANK HE'S NOT USING...
IS THAT... THE NINJA CAT?
CLAU...UH, YEAH, IT'S CAT NINJA, MOM.
THANKS, CAT NINJA!
VROOOOOOOOOM

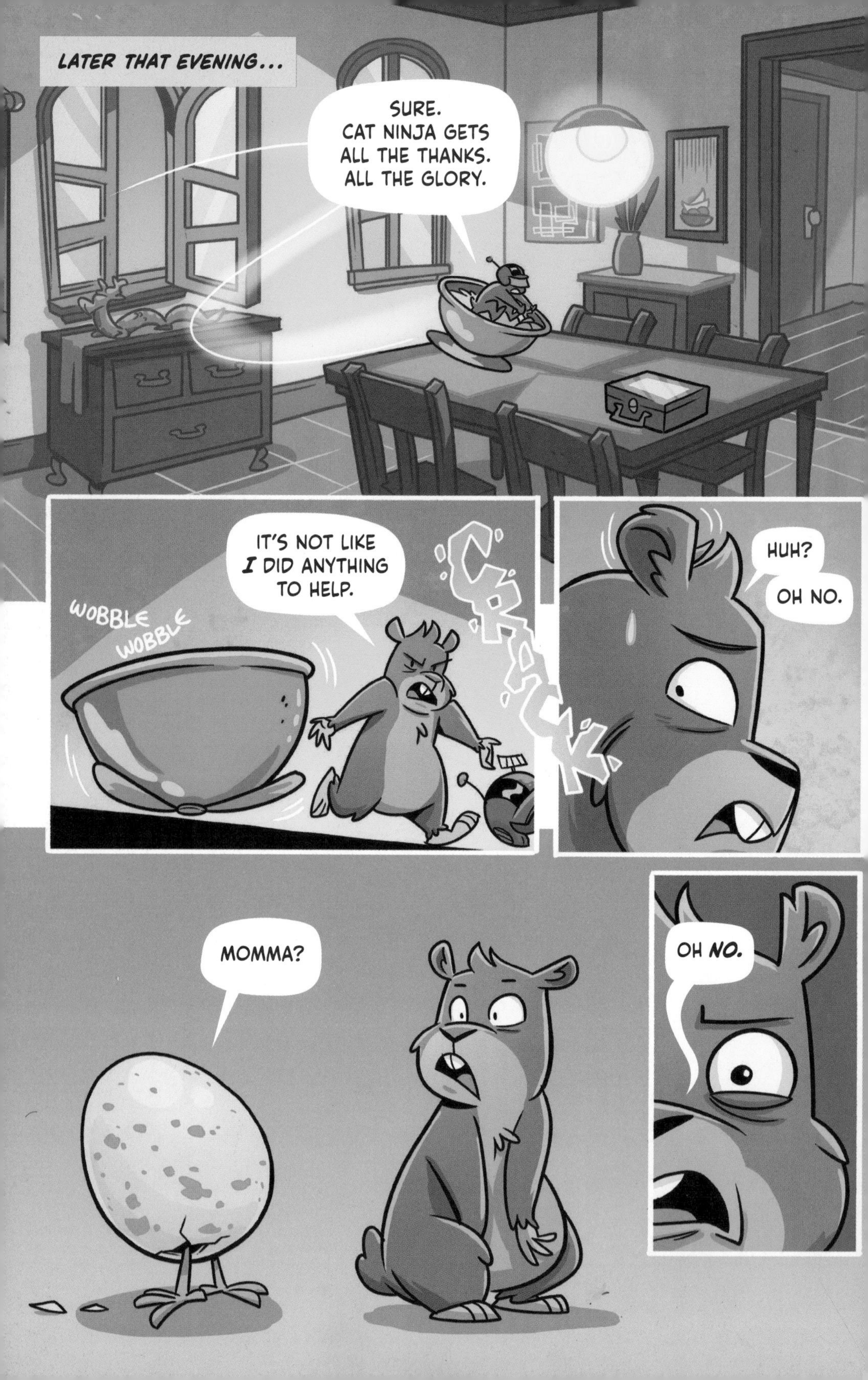
LATER THAT EVENING...
SURE. CAT NINJA GETS ALL THE THANKS. ALL THE GLORY.
IT'S NOT LIKE *I* DID ANYTHING TO HELP.
WOBBLE WOBBLE
CRACK
HUH?
OH NO.
MOMMA?
OH *NO.*

Chapter 2: *Baby's Day Out*

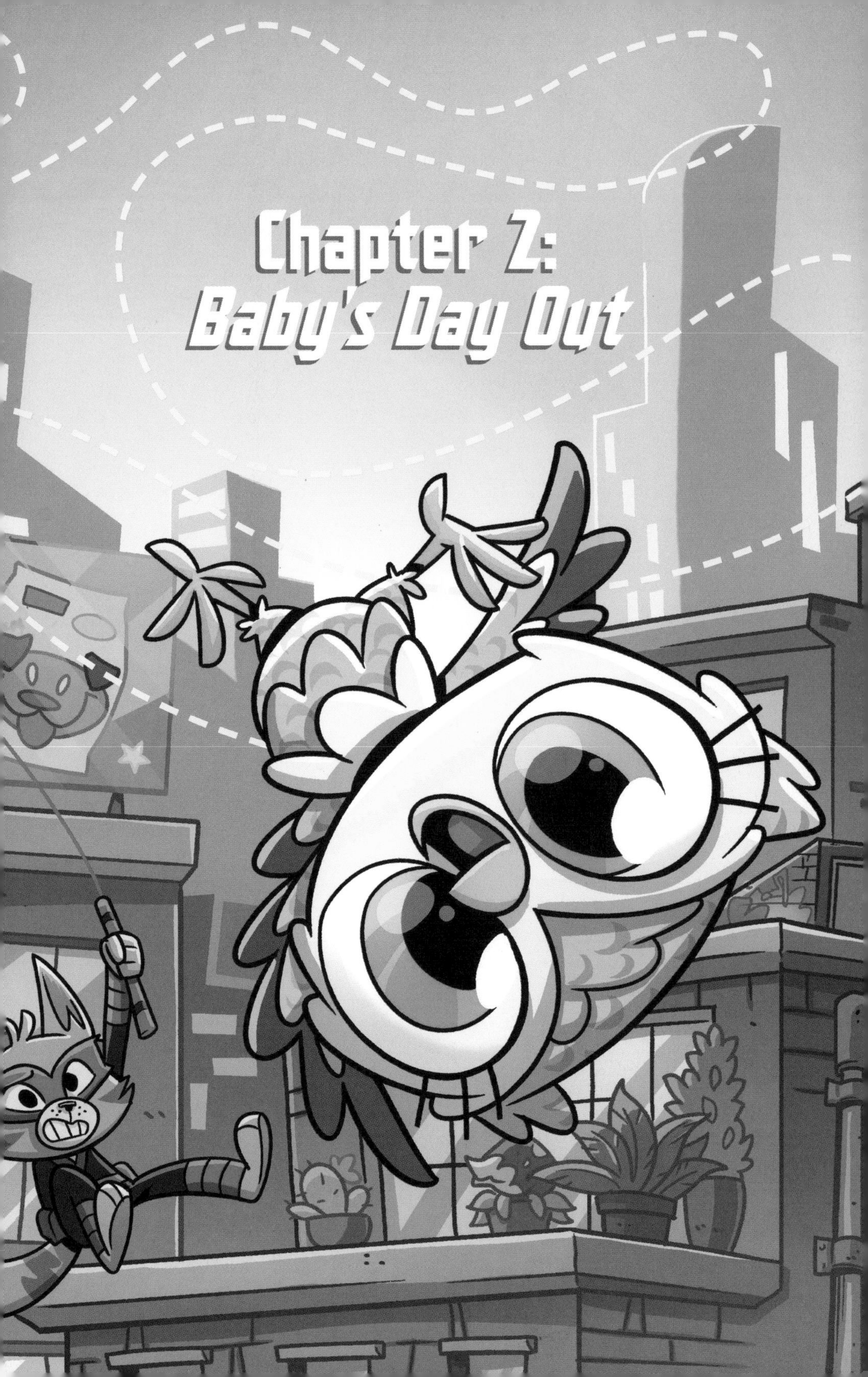

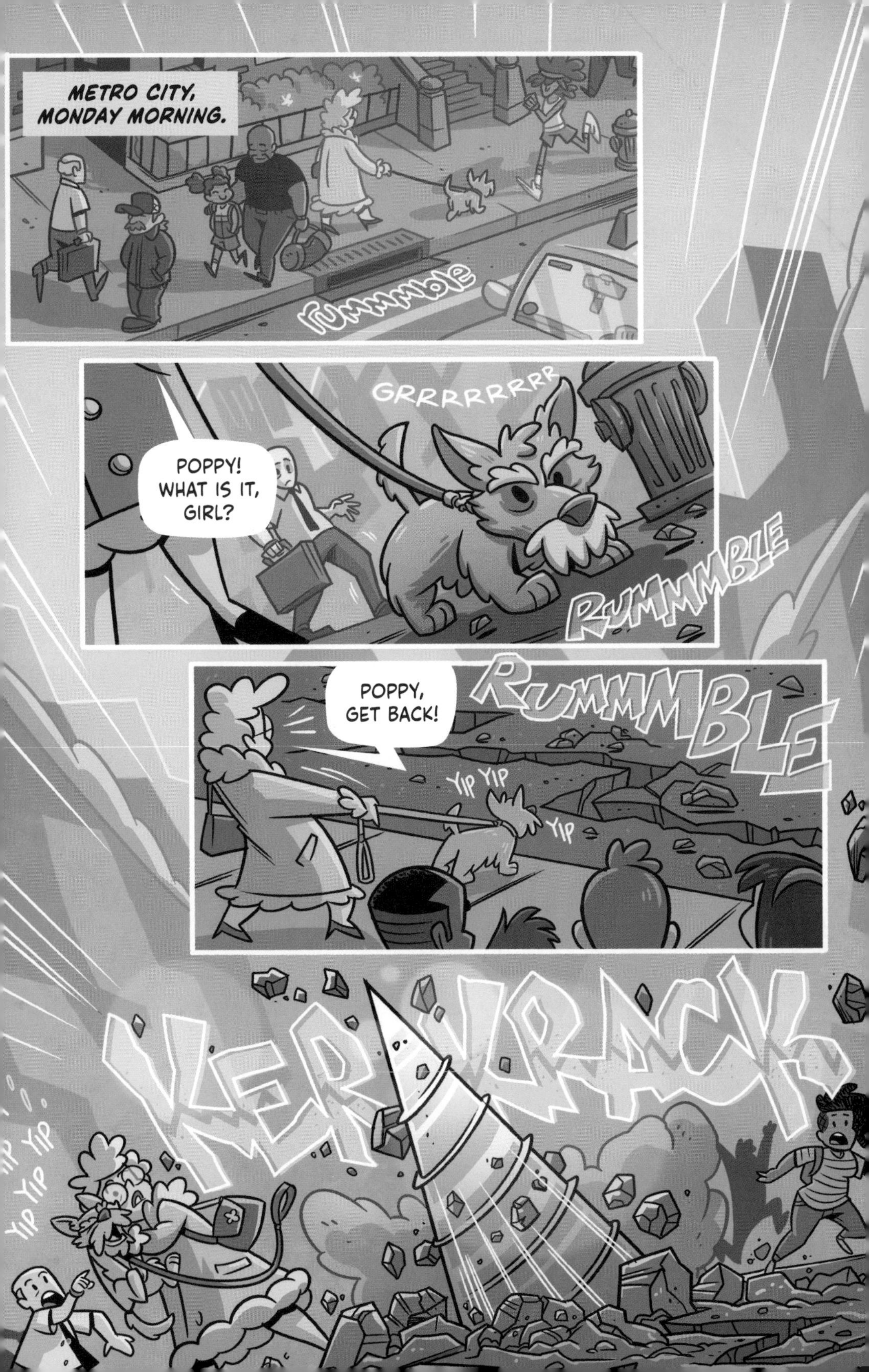
METRO CITY, MONDAY MORNING.
RUMMMBLE
GRRRRRRRR
POPPY! WHAT IS IT, GIRL?
RUMMMBLE
POPPY, GET BACK!
RUMMMBLE
YIP YIP
YIP
KERVRACK
YIP YIP
YIP YIP

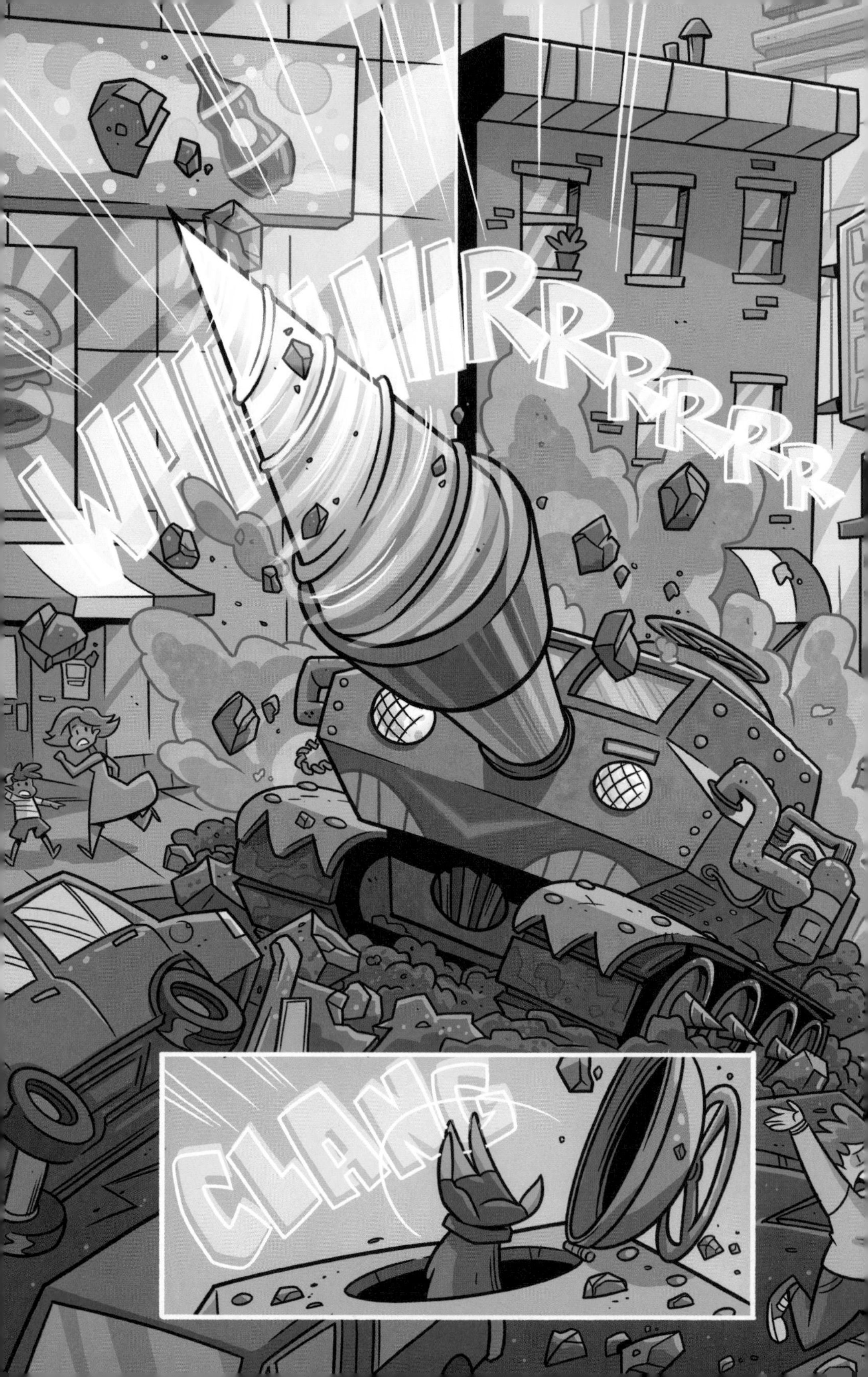
WHHHHIIIRRRRRRRRR
CLANG

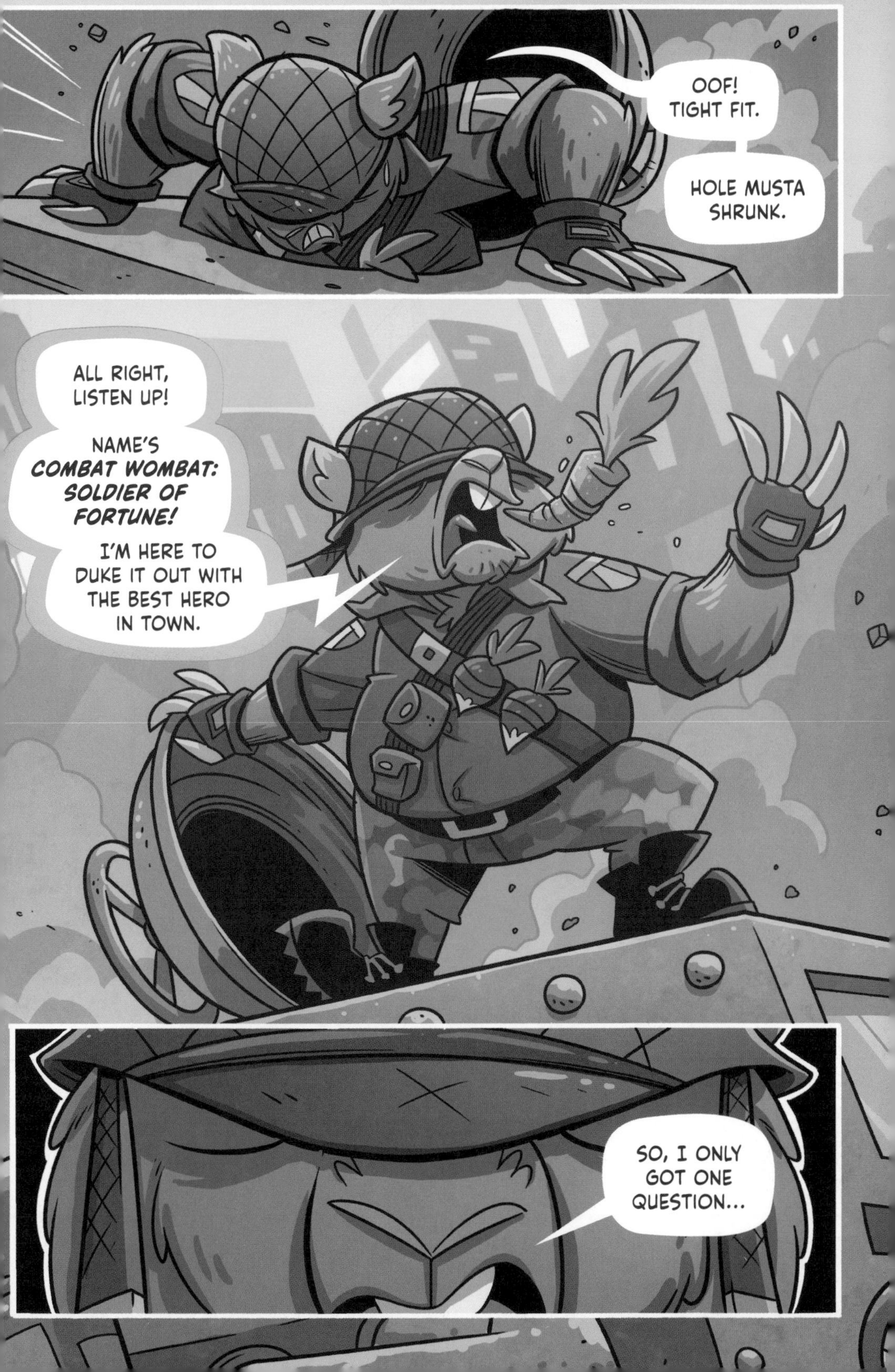
OOF! TIGHT FIT.
HOLE MUSTA SHRUNK.
ALL RIGHT, LISTEN UP!
NAME'S *COMBAT WOMBAT: SOLDIER OF FORTUNE!*
I'M HERE TO DUKE IT OUT WITH THE BEST HERO IN TOWN.
SO, I ONLY GOT ONE QUESTION...

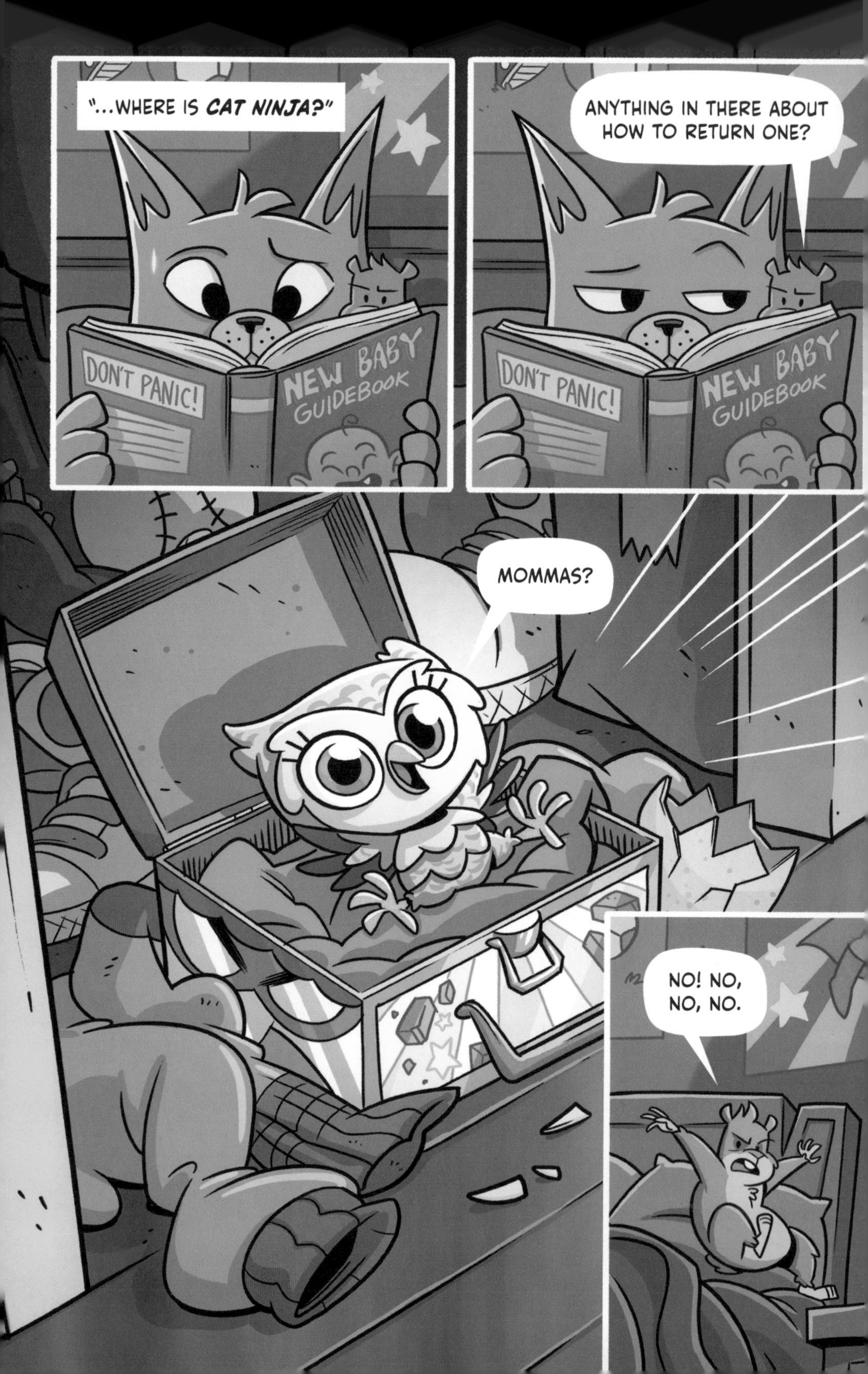

"...WHERE IS *CAT NINJA?*"
DON'T PANIC!
NEW BABY GUIDEBOOK
ANYTHING IN THERE ABOUT HOW TO RETURN ONE?
DON'T PANIC!
NEW BABY GUIDEBOOK
MOMMAS?
NO! NO, NO, NO.

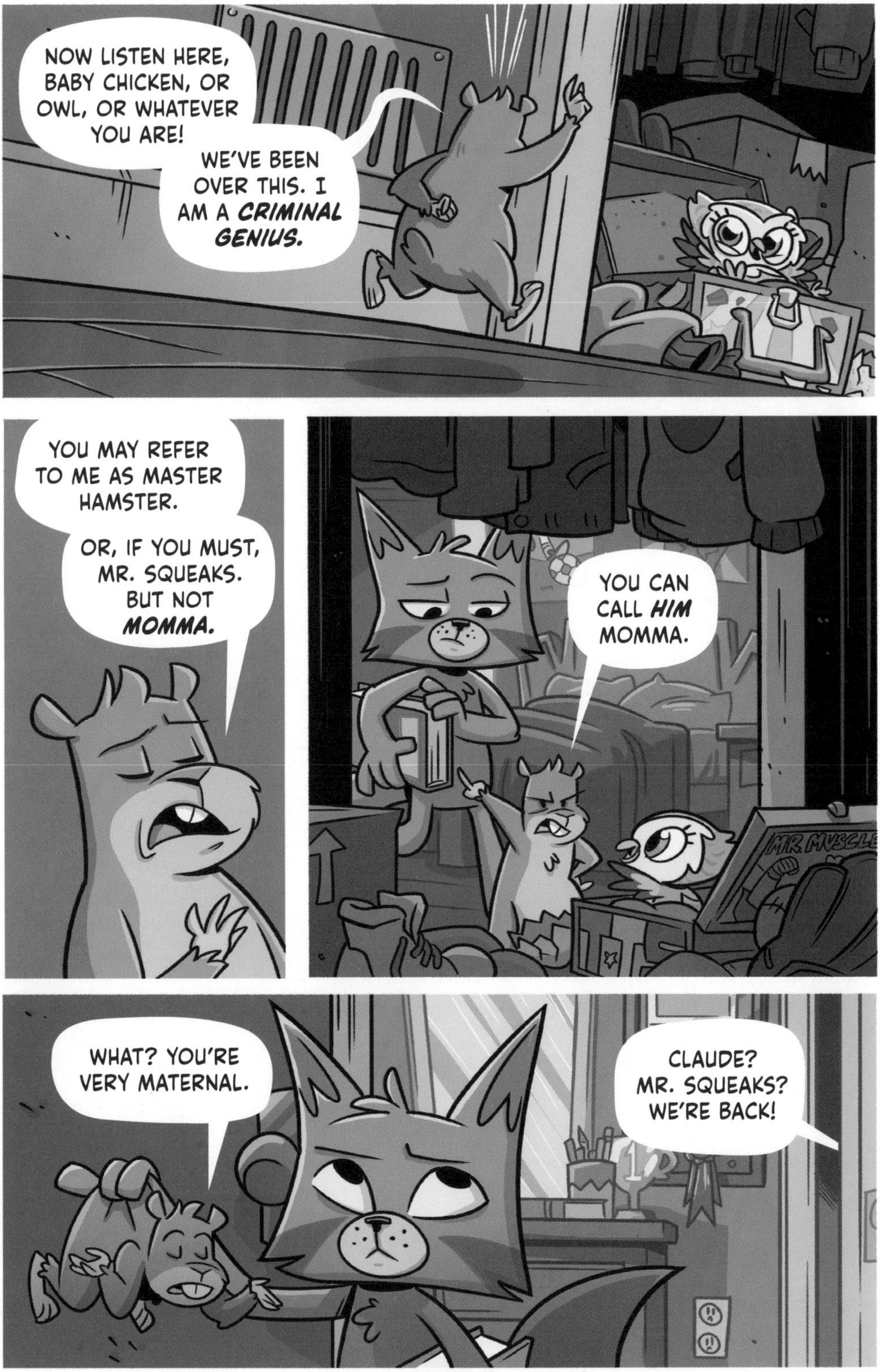
NOW LISTEN HERE, BABY CHICKEN, OR OWL, OR WHATEVER YOU ARE!
WE'VE BEEN OVER THIS. I AM A *CRIMINAL GENIUS.*
YOU MAY REFER TO ME AS MASTER HAMSTER.
OR, IF YOU MUST, MR. SQUEAKS. BUT NOT *MOMMA.*
YOU CAN CALL *HIM* MOMMA.
MR. MUSCLE
WHAT? YOU'RE VERY MATERNAL.
CLAUDE? MR. SQUEAKS? WE'RE BACK!

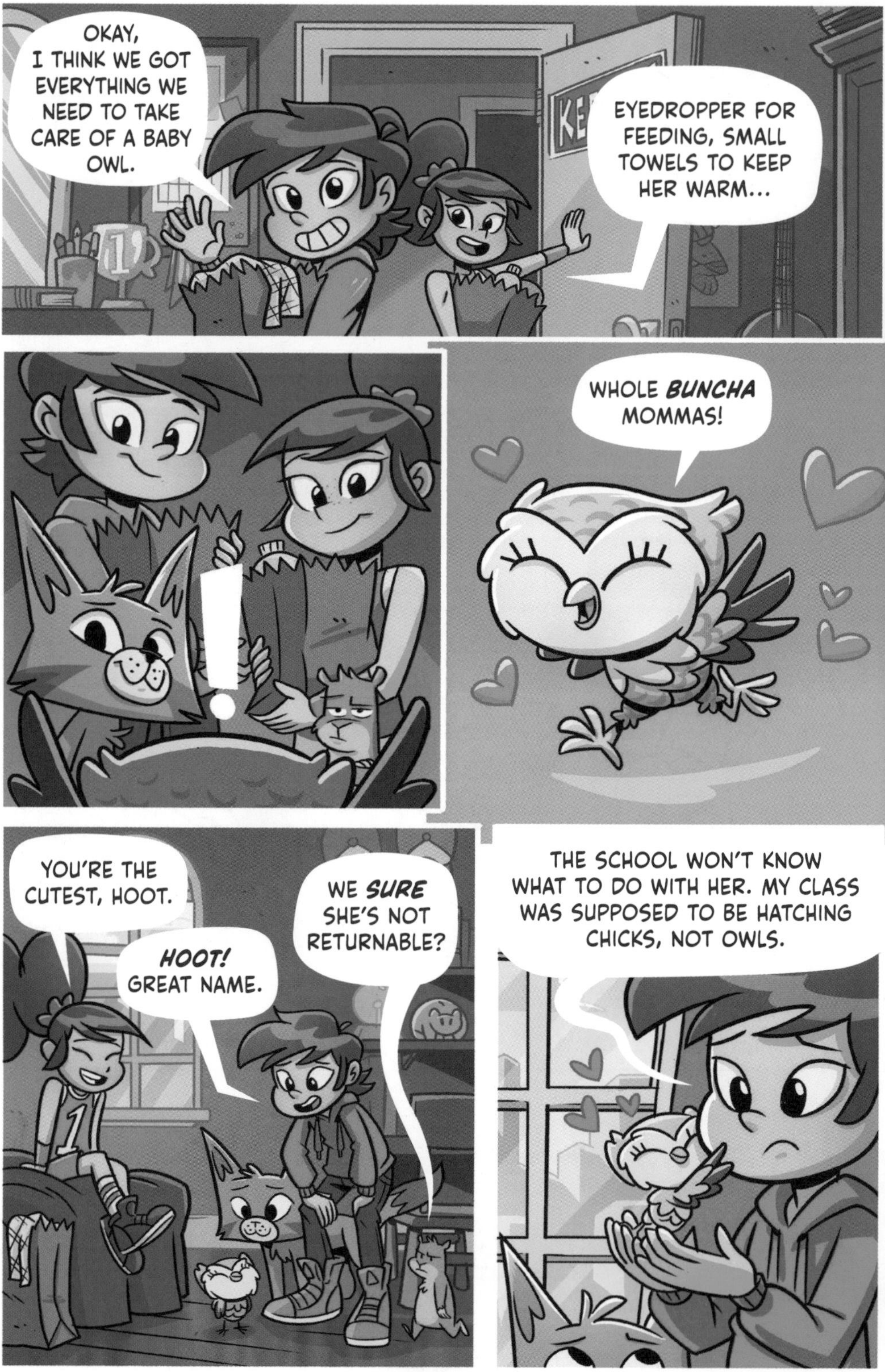
OKAY, I THINK WE GOT EVERYTHING WE NEED TO TAKE CARE OF A BABY OWL.
EYEDROPPER FOR FEEDING, SMALL TOWELS TO KEEP HER WARM...
WHOLE **BUNCHA** MOMMAS!
YOU'RE THE CUTEST, HOOT.
HOOT! GREAT NAME.
WE **SURE** SHE'S NOT RETURNABLE?
THE SCHOOL WON'T KNOW WHAT TO DO WITH HER. MY CLASS WAS SUPPOSED TO BE HATCHING CHICKS, NOT OWLS.

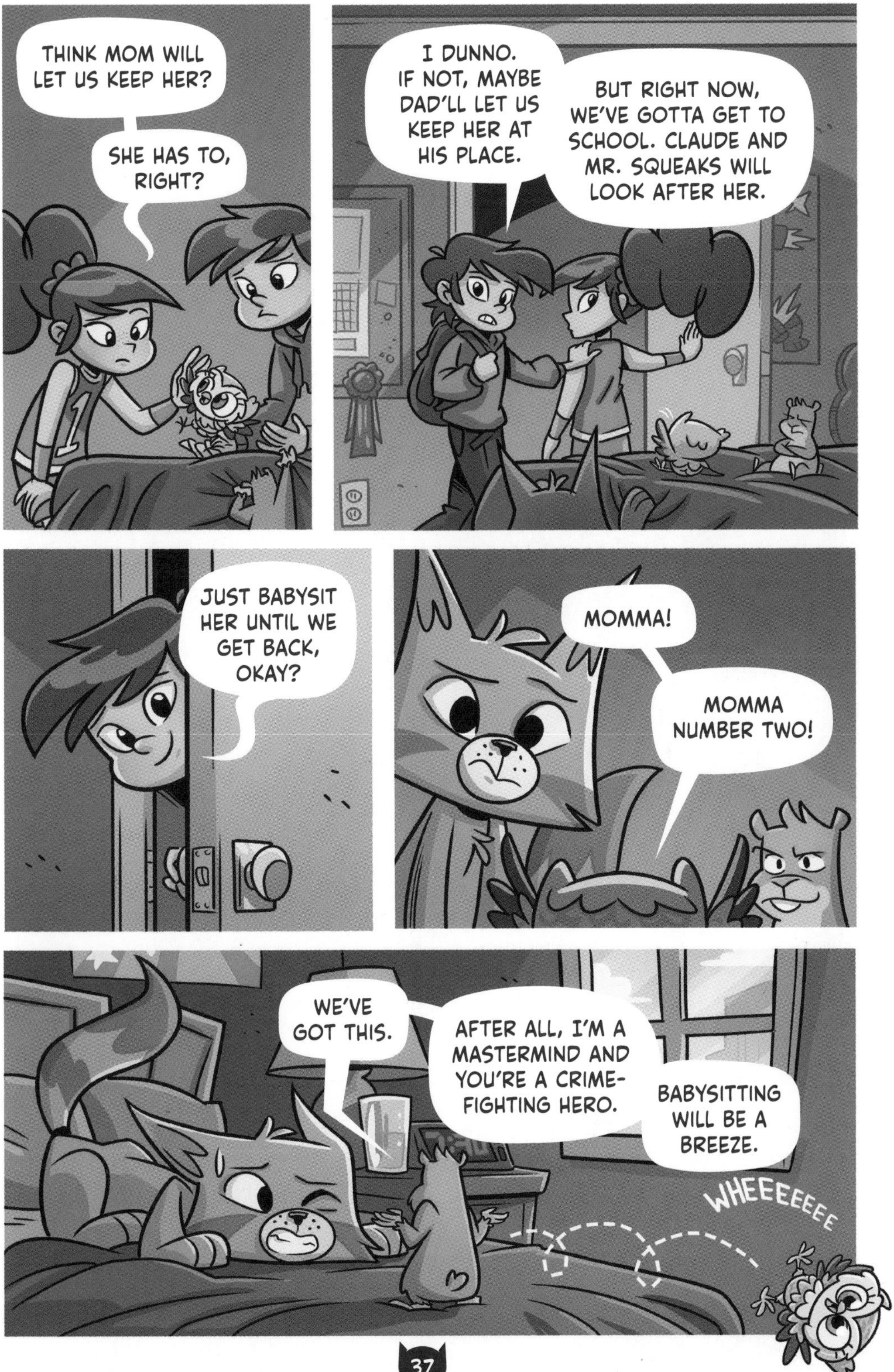
THINK MOM WILL LET US KEEP HER?
SHE HAS TO, RIGHT?
I DUNNO. IF NOT, MAYBE DAD'LL LET US KEEP HER AT HIS PLACE.
BUT RIGHT NOW, WE'VE GOTTA GET TO SCHOOL. CLAUDE AND MR. SQUEAKS WILL LOOK AFTER HER.
JUST BABYSIT HER UNTIL WE GET BACK, OKAY?
MOMMA!
MOMMA NUMBER TWO!
WE'VE GOT THIS.
AFTER ALL, I'M A MASTERMIND AND YOU'RE A CRIME-FIGHTING HERO.
BABYSITTING WILL BE A BREEZE.
WHEEEEEEE

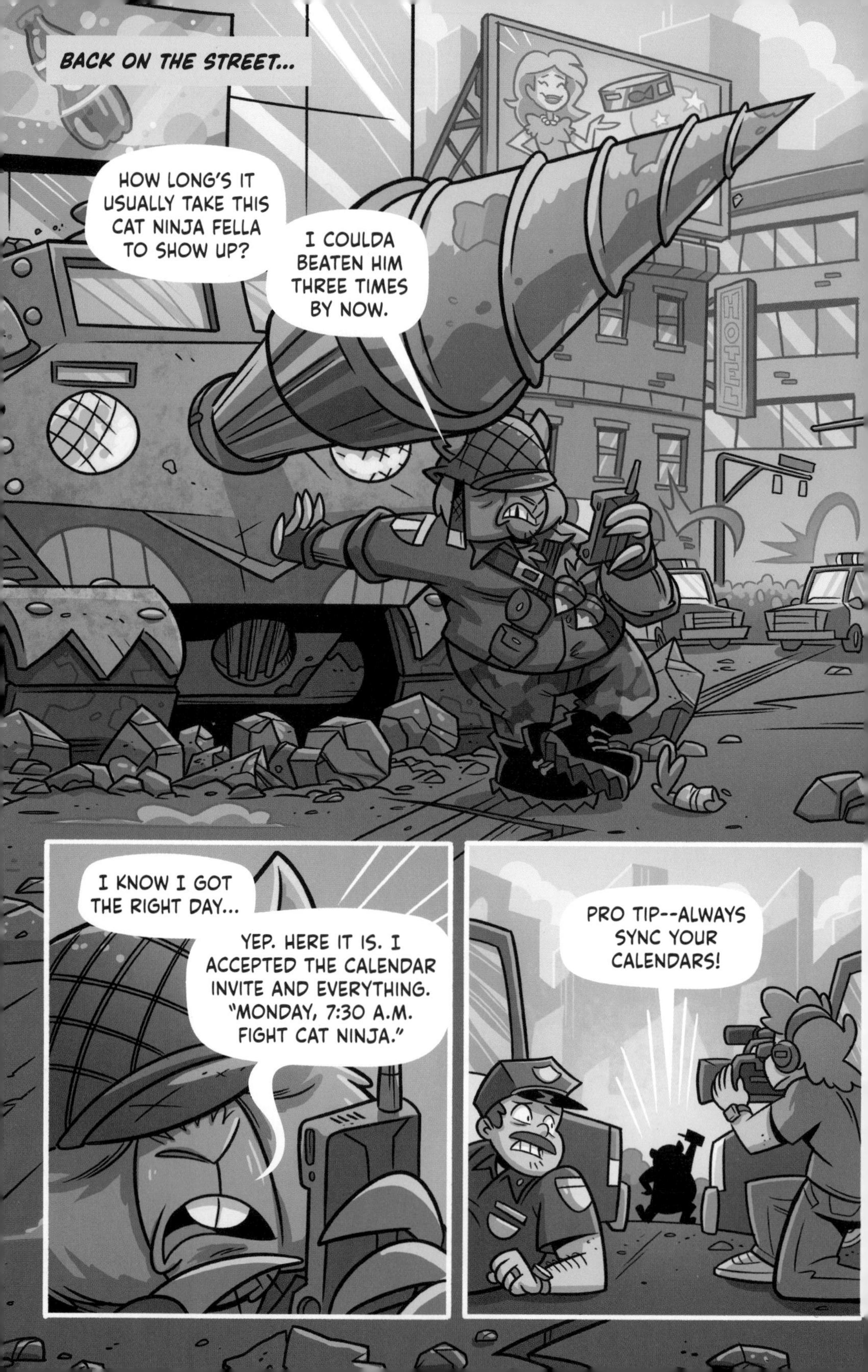
BACK ON THE STREET...
HOW LONG'S IT USUALLY TAKE THIS CAT NINJA FELLA TO SHOW UP?
I COULDA BEATEN HIM THREE TIMES BY NOW.
HOTEL
I KNOW I GOT THE RIGHT DAY...
YEP. HERE IT IS. I ACCEPTED THE CALENDAR INVITE AND EVERYTHING. "MONDAY, 7:30 A.M. FIGHT CAT NINJA."
PRO TIP--ALWAYS SYNC YOUR CALENDARS!

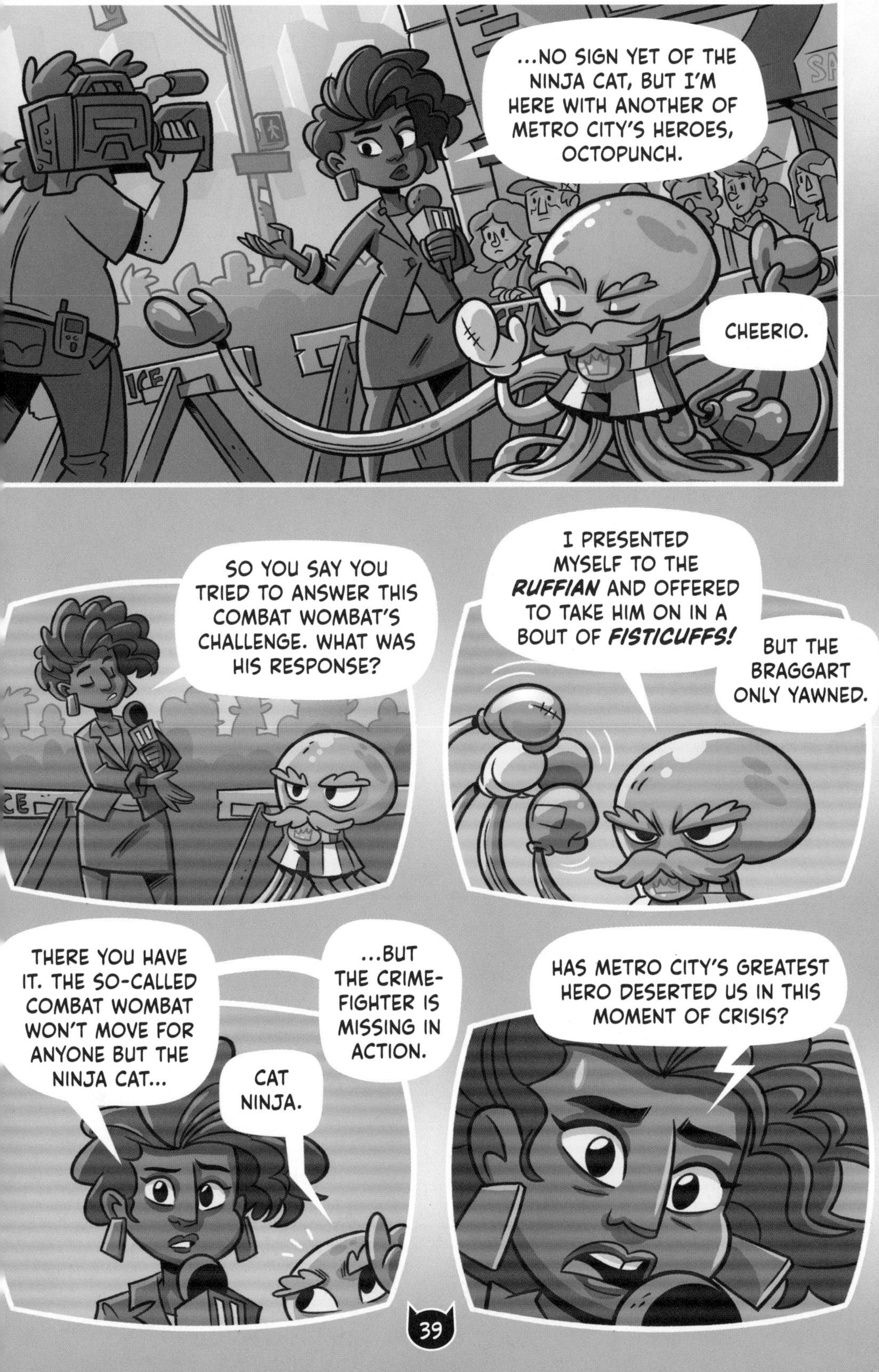

...NO SIGN YET OF THE NINJA CAT, BUT I'M HERE WITH ANOTHER OF METRO CITY'S HEROES, OCTOPUNCH.
CHEERIO.
SO YOU SAY YOU TRIED TO ANSWER THIS COMBAT WOMBAT'S CHALLENGE. WHAT WAS HIS RESPONSE?
I PRESENTED MYSELF TO THE *RUFFIAN* AND OFFERED TO TAKE HIM ON IN A BOUT OF *FISTICUFFS!*
BUT THE BRAGGART ONLY YAWNED.
THERE YOU HAVE IT. THE SO-CALLED COMBAT WOMBAT WON'T MOVE FOR ANYONE BUT THE NINJA CAT...
...BUT THE CRIME-FIGHTER IS MISSING IN ACTION.
CAT NINJA.
HAS METRO CITY'S GREATEST HERO DESERTED US IN THIS MOMENT OF CRISIS?

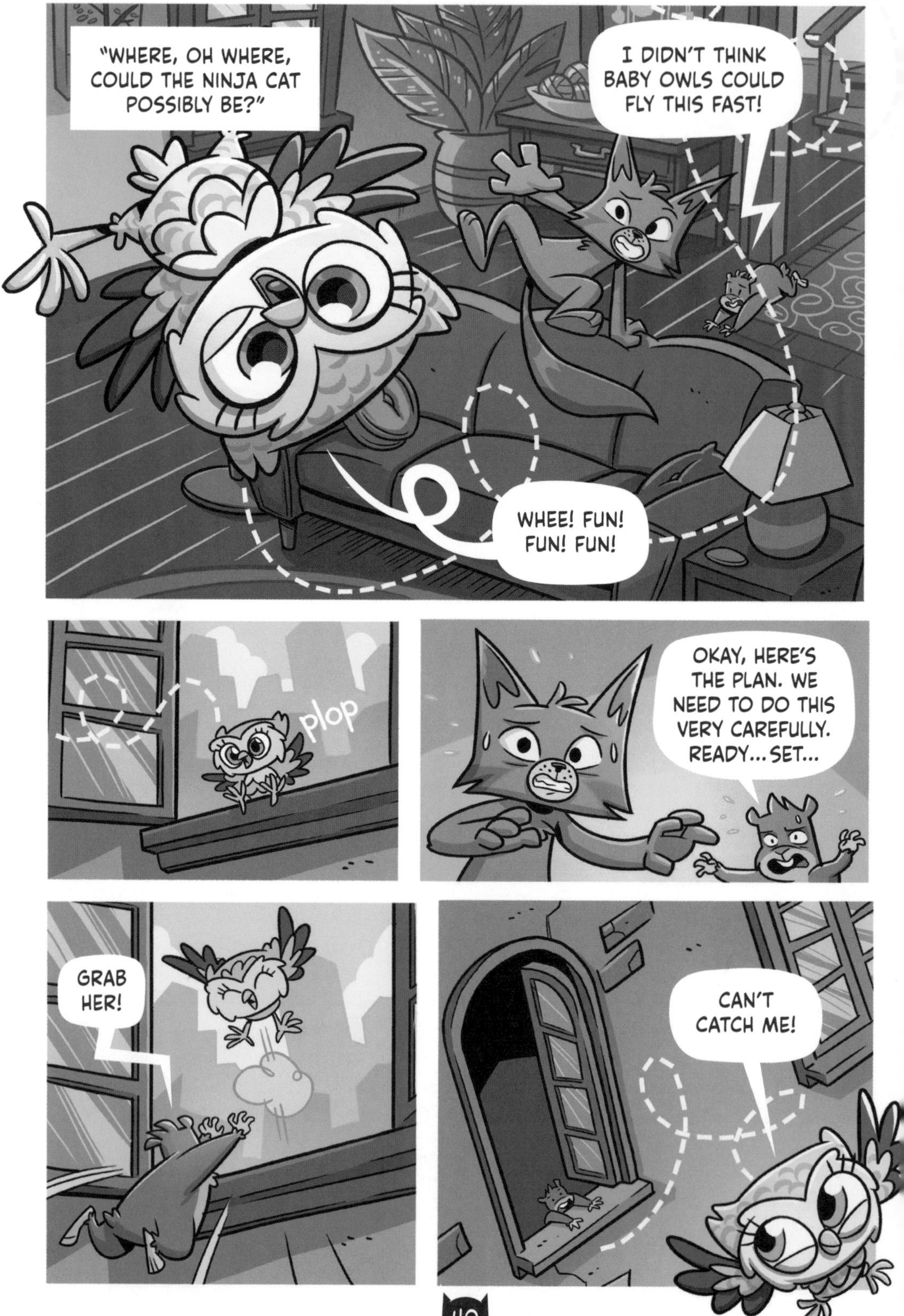
"WHERE, OH WHERE, COULD THE NINJA CAT POSSIBLY BE?"
I DIDN'T THINK BABY OWLS COULD FLY THIS FAST!
WHEE! FUN! FUN! FUN!
plop
OKAY, HERE'S THE PLAN. WE NEED TO DO THIS VERY CAREFULLY. READY... SET...
GRAB HER!
CAN'T CATCH ME!

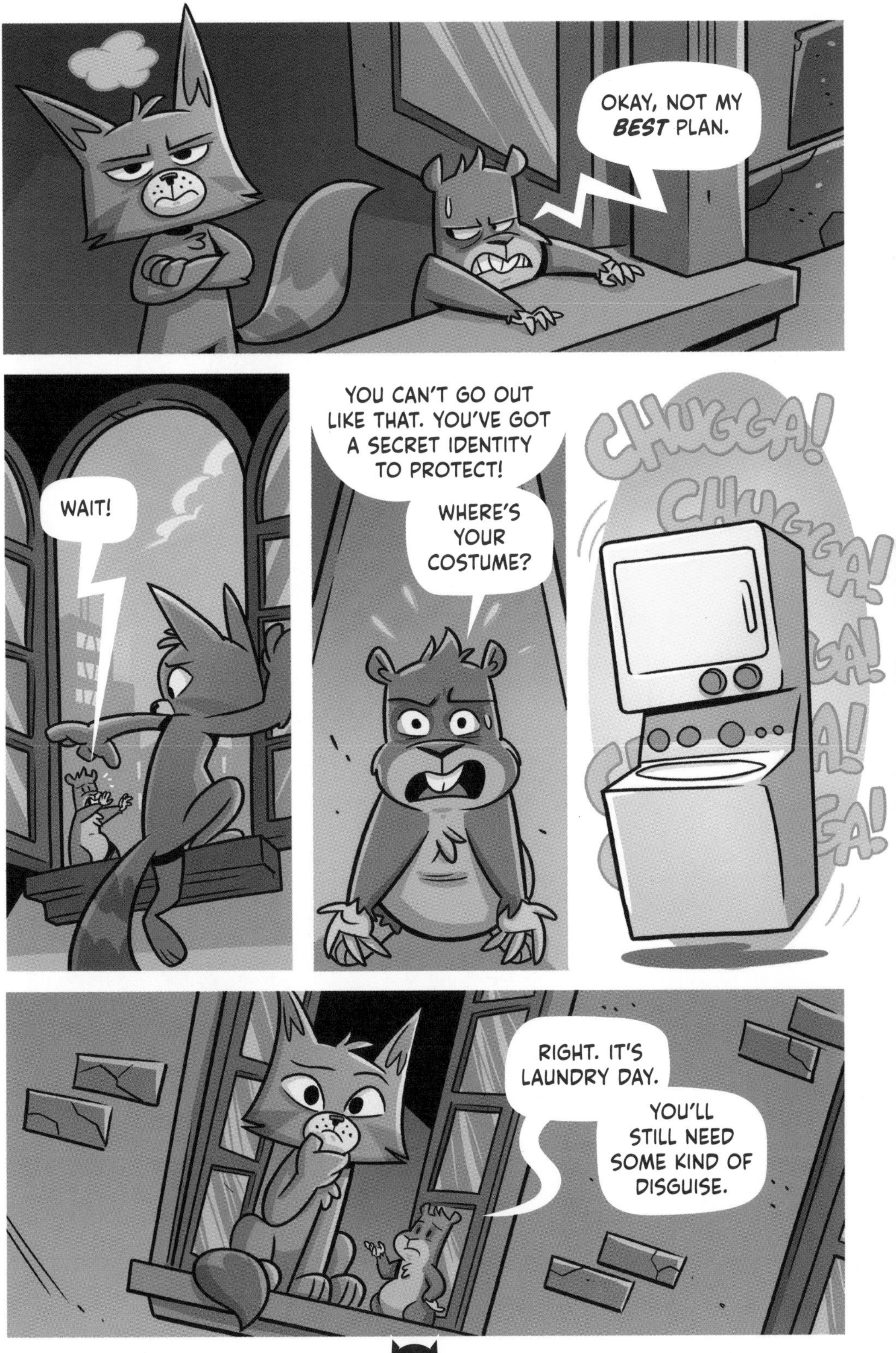
OKAY, NOT MY *BEST* PLAN.
WAIT!
YOU CAN'T GO OUT LIKE THAT. YOU'VE GOT A SECRET IDENTITY TO PROTECT!
WHERE'S YOUR COSTUME?
CHUGGA! CHUGGA!
RIGHT. IT'S LAUNDRY DAY.
YOU'LL STILL NEED SOME KIND OF DISGUISE.

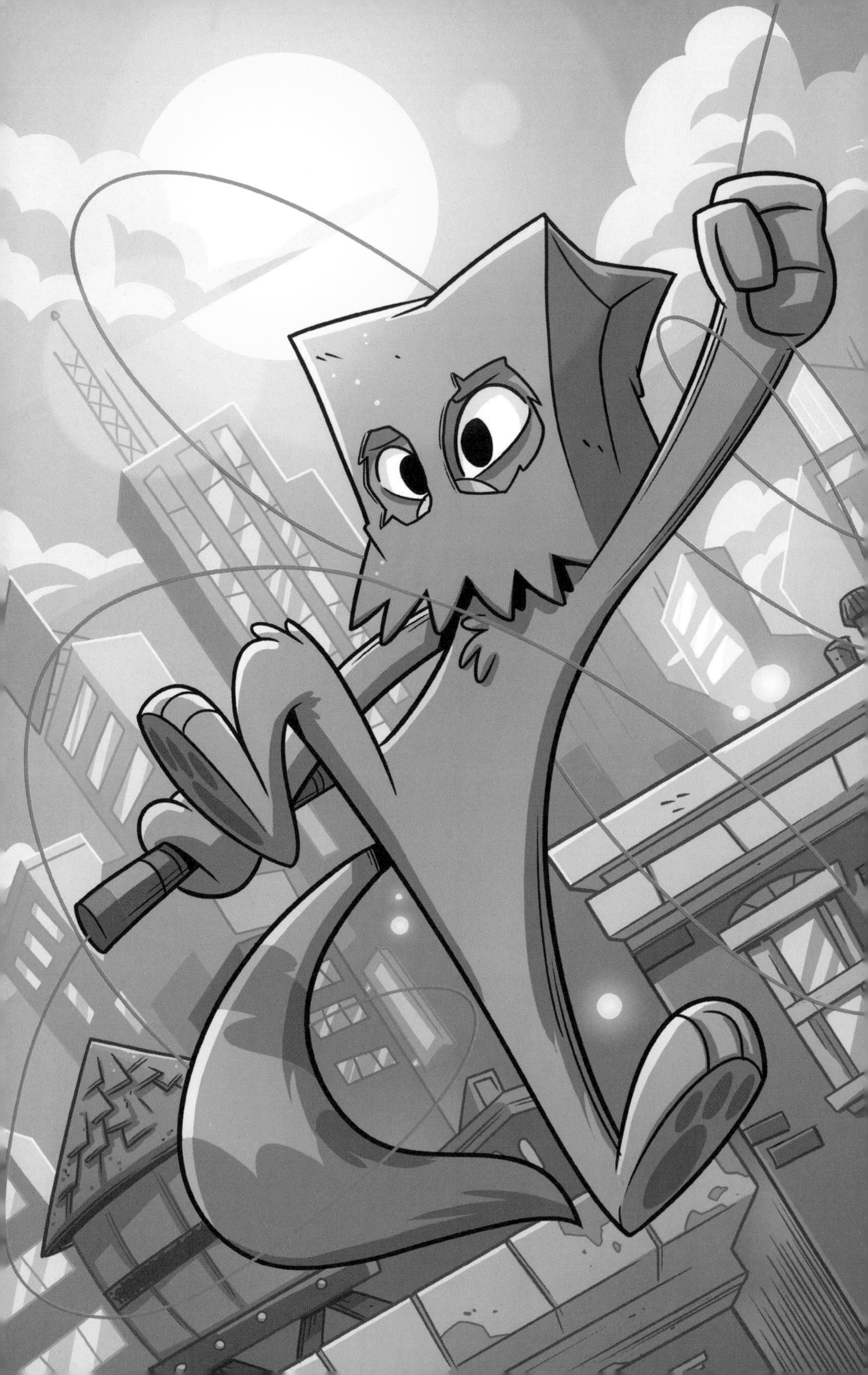

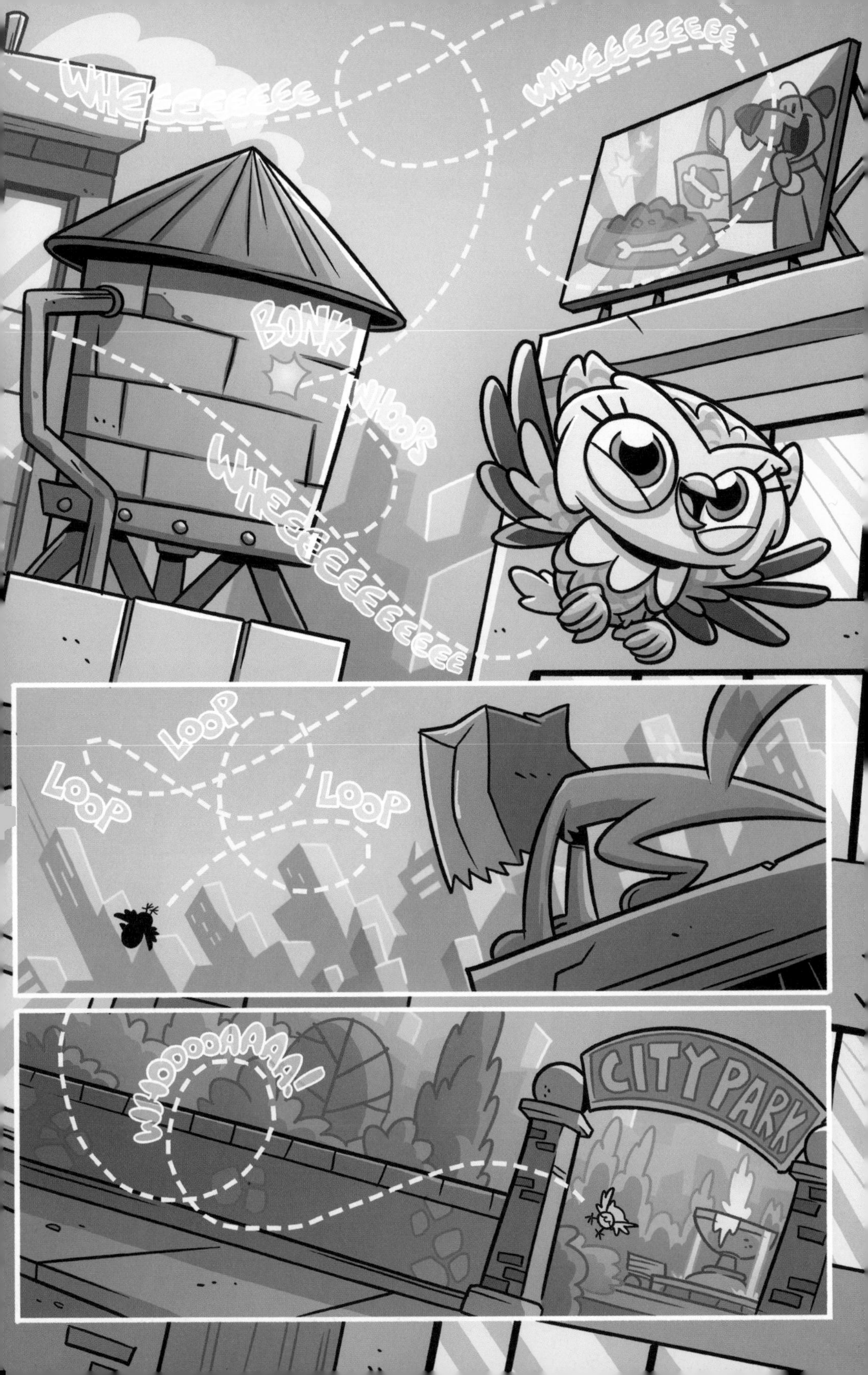
WHEEEEEEE
WHEEEEEEEEEE
BONK
WHOOPS
WHEEEEEEEEEEE
LOOP
LOOP
LOOP
WHOOOOAAAAA!
CITY PARK

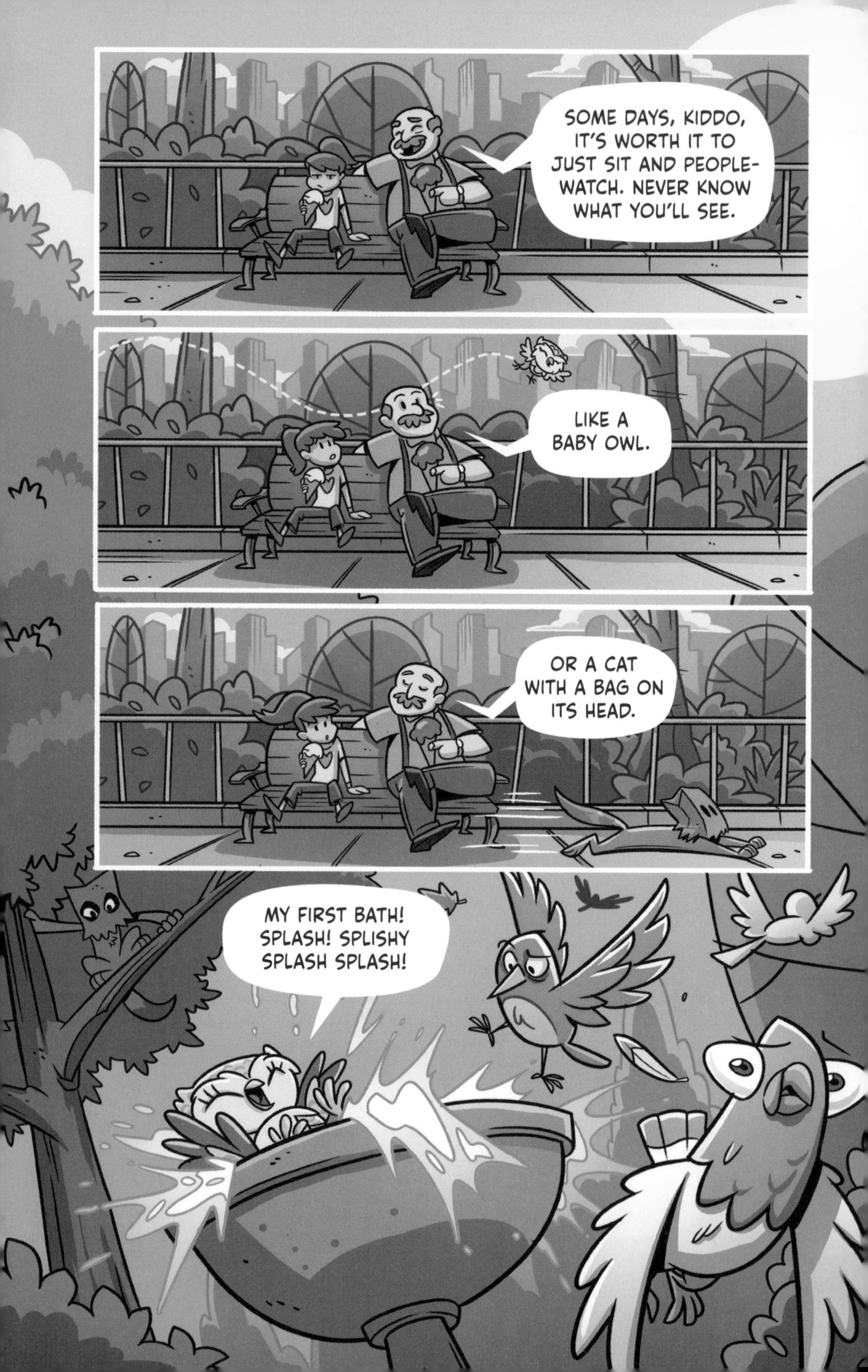
SOME DAYS, KIDDO, IT'S WORTH IT TO JUST SIT AND PEOPLE-WATCH. NEVER KNOW WHAT YOU'LL SEE.
LIKE A BABY OWL.
OR A CAT WITH A BAG ON ITS HEAD.
MY FIRST BATH! SPLASH! SPLISHY SPLASH SPLASH!

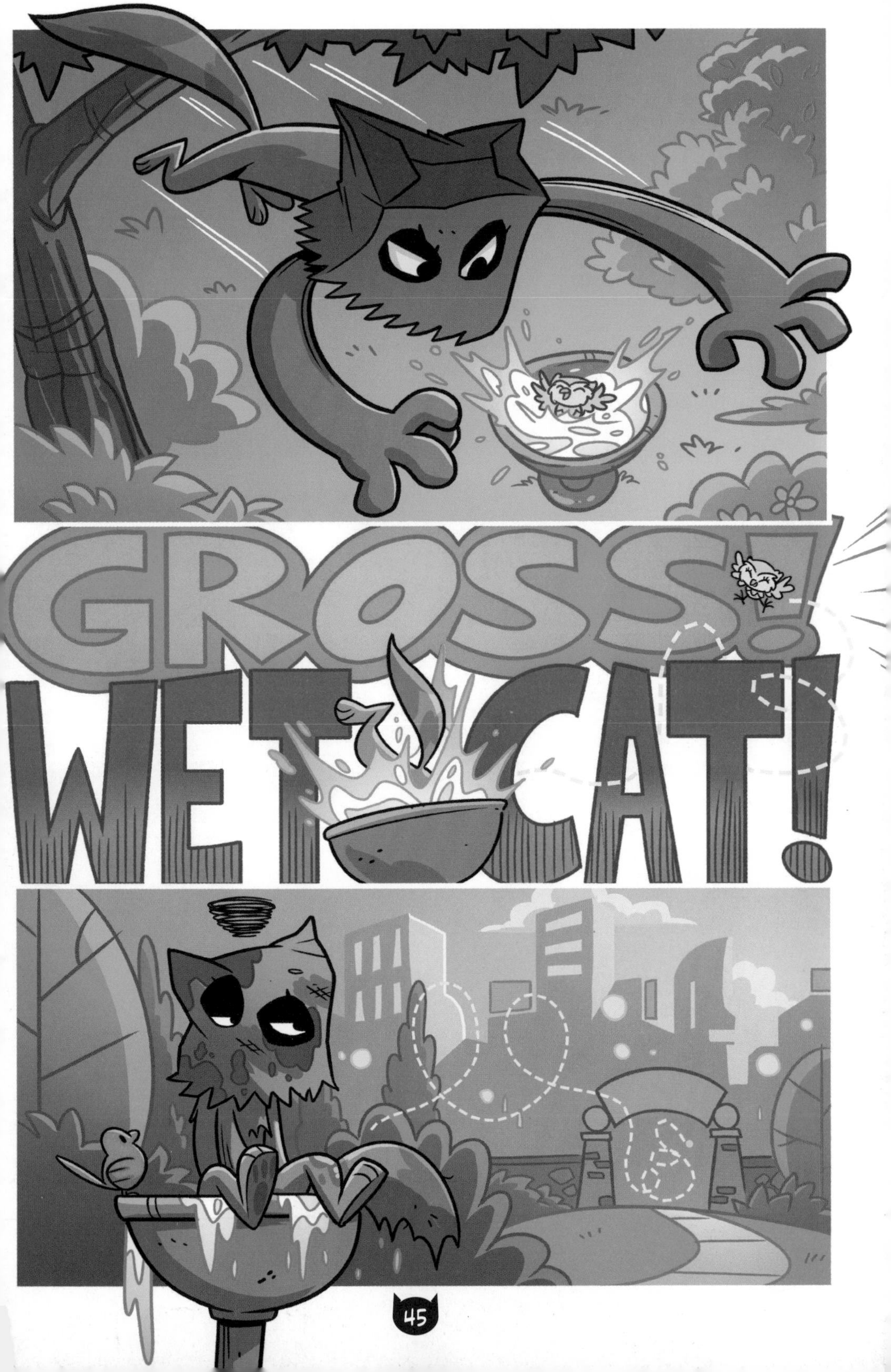
GROSS!
WET CAT!

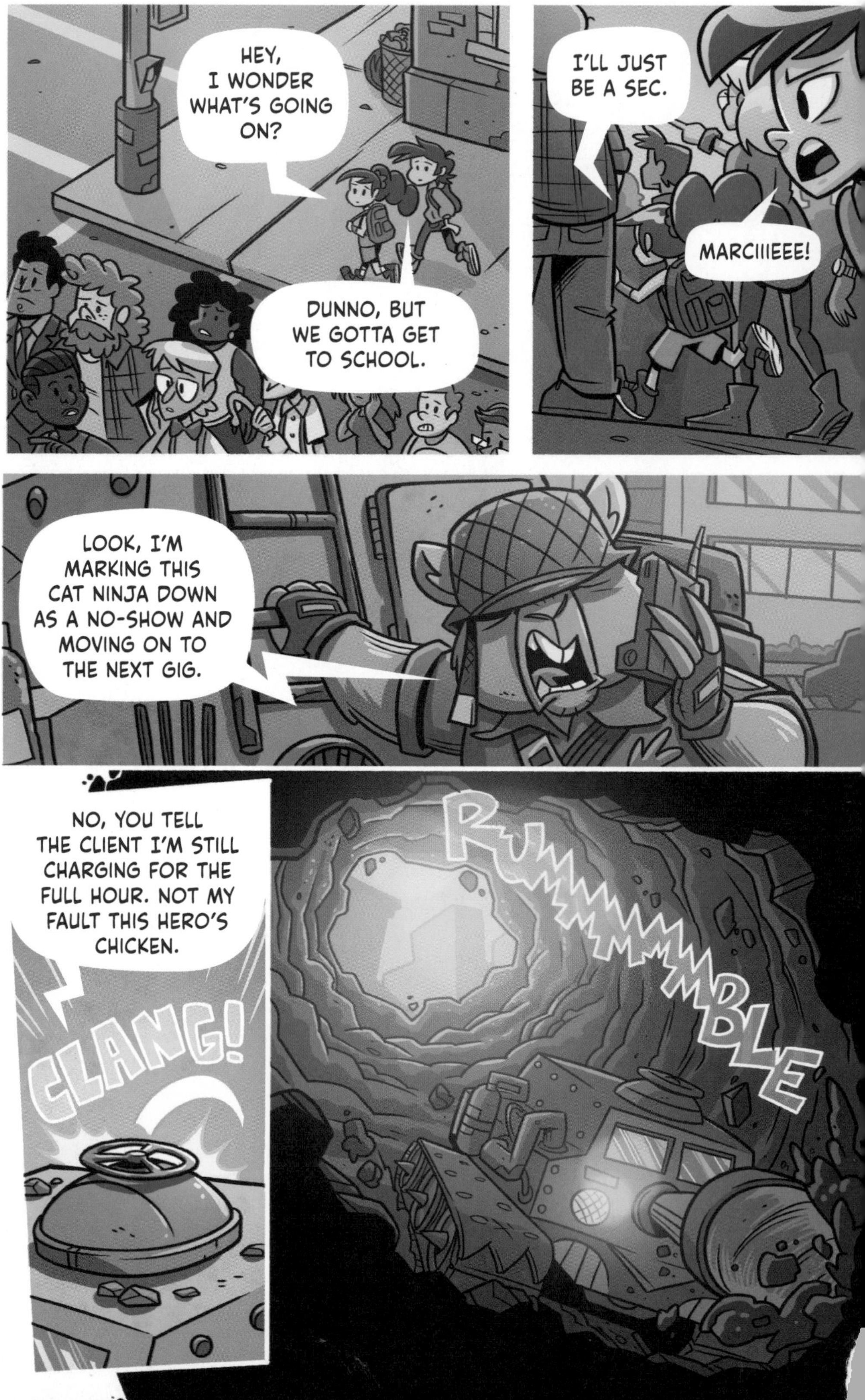
HEY, I WONDER WHAT'S GOING ON?
DUNNO, BUT WE GOTTA GET TO SCHOOL.
I'LL JUST BE A SEC.
MARCIIIEEE!
LOOK, I'M MARKING THIS CAT NINJA DOWN AS A NO-SHOW AND MOVING ON TO THE NEXT GIG.
NO, YOU TELL THE CLIENT I'M STILL CHARGING FOR THE FULL HOUR. NOT MY FAULT THIS HERO'S CHICKEN.
CLANG!
RUMMMMMBLE

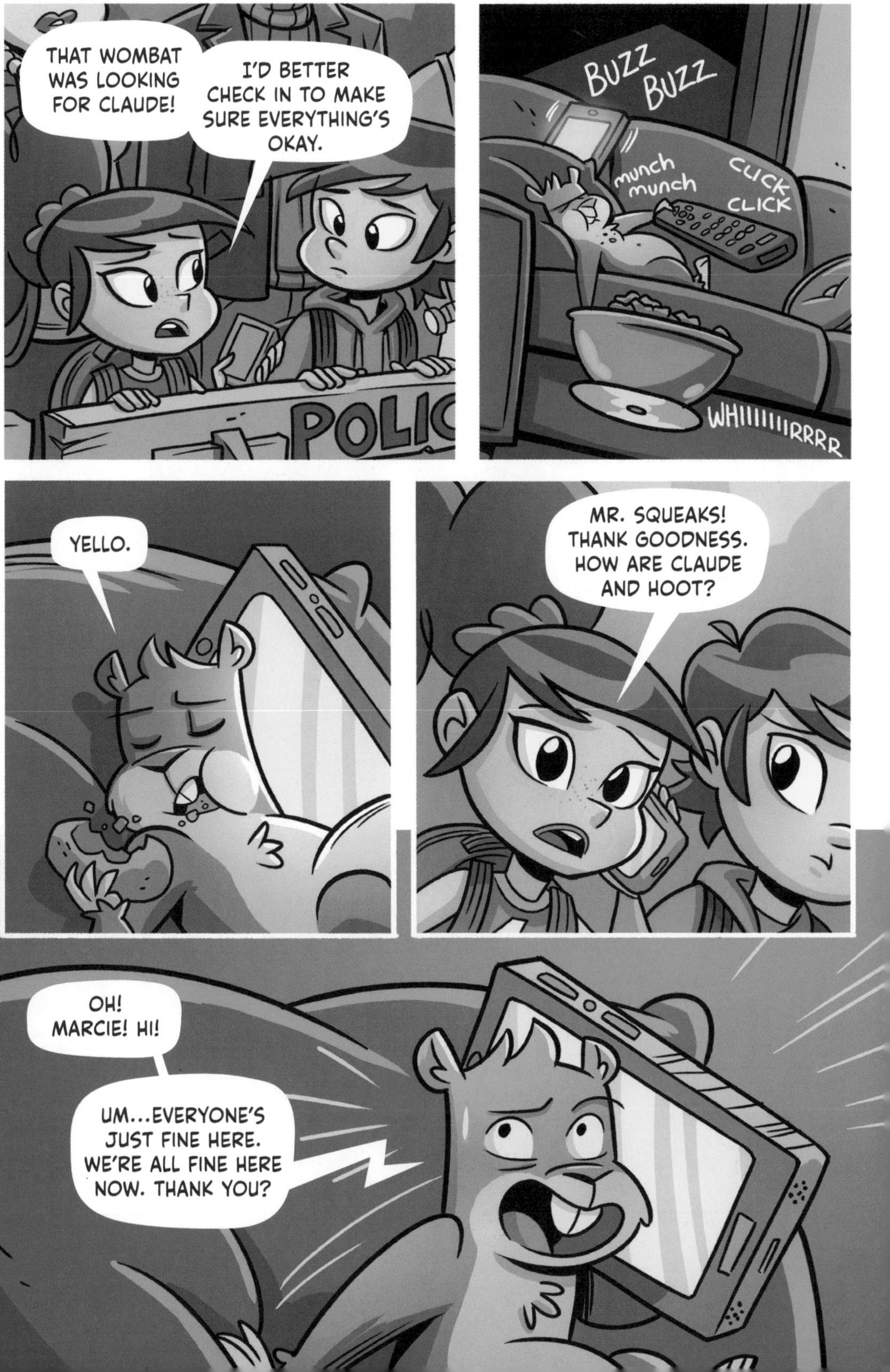
THAT WOMBAT WAS LOOKING FOR CLAUDE!
I'D BETTER CHECK IN TO MAKE SURE EVERYTHING'S OKAY.
POLIC
BUZZ BUZZ
munch munch
CLICK CLICK
WHIIIIIIIRRRR
YELLO.
MR. SQUEAKS! THANK GOODNESS. HOW ARE CLAUDE AND HOOT?
OH! MARCIE! HI!
UM...EVERYONE'S JUST FINE HERE. WE'RE ALL FINE HERE NOW. THANK YOU?

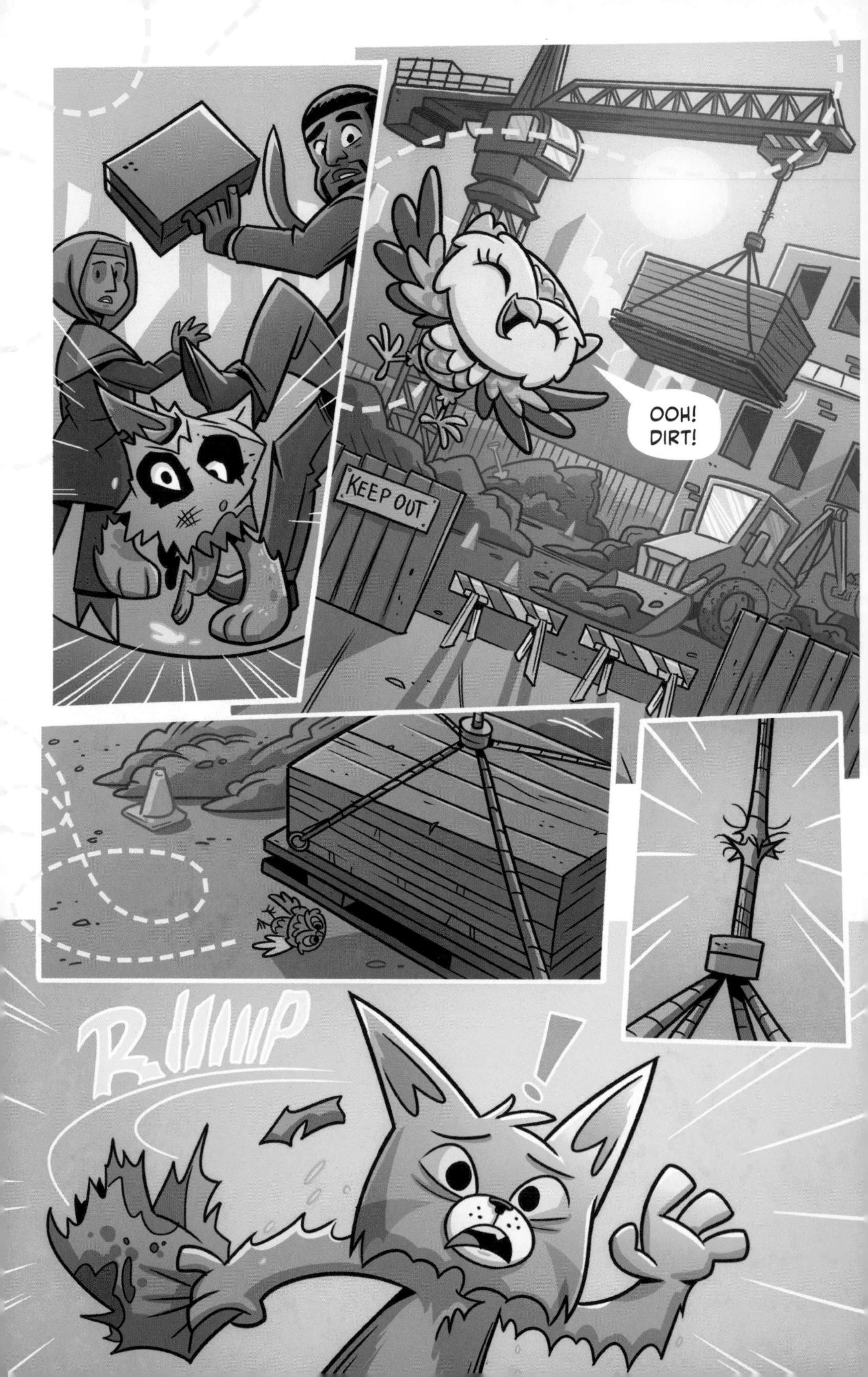
OOH!
DIRT!
KEEP OUT
RIIIIP

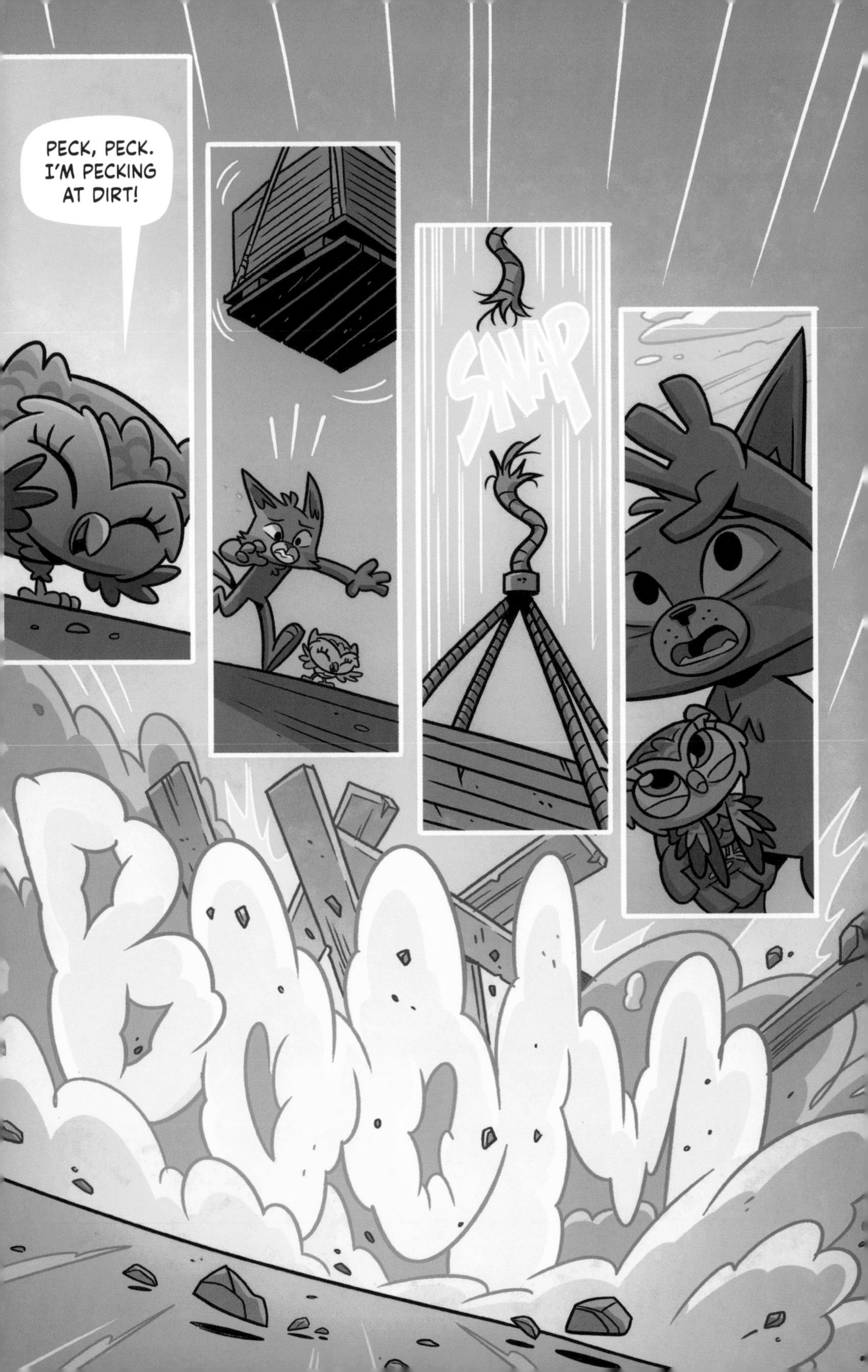
PECK, PECK. I'M PECKING AT DIRT!
SNAP
BOOOM

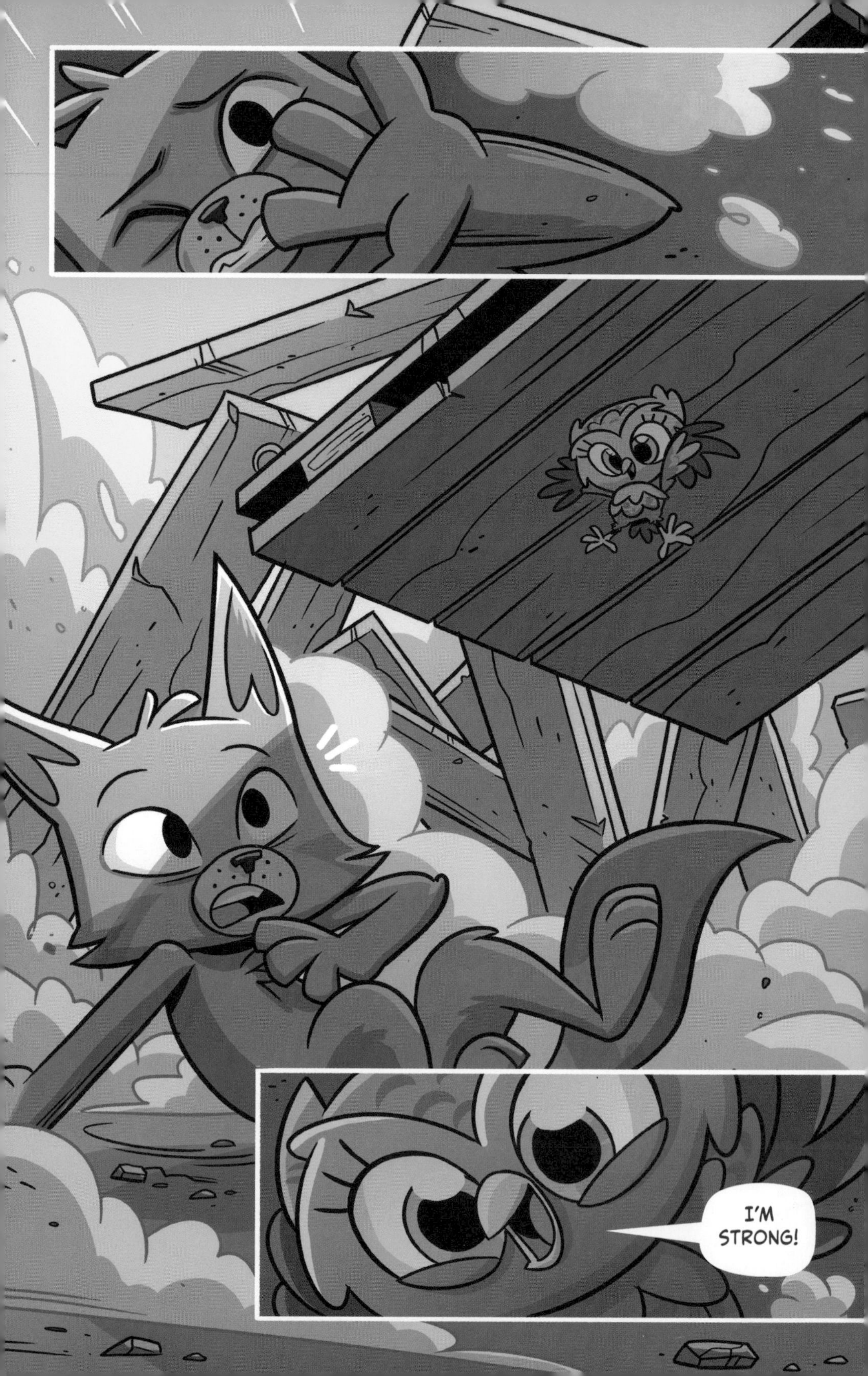
I'M
STRONG!

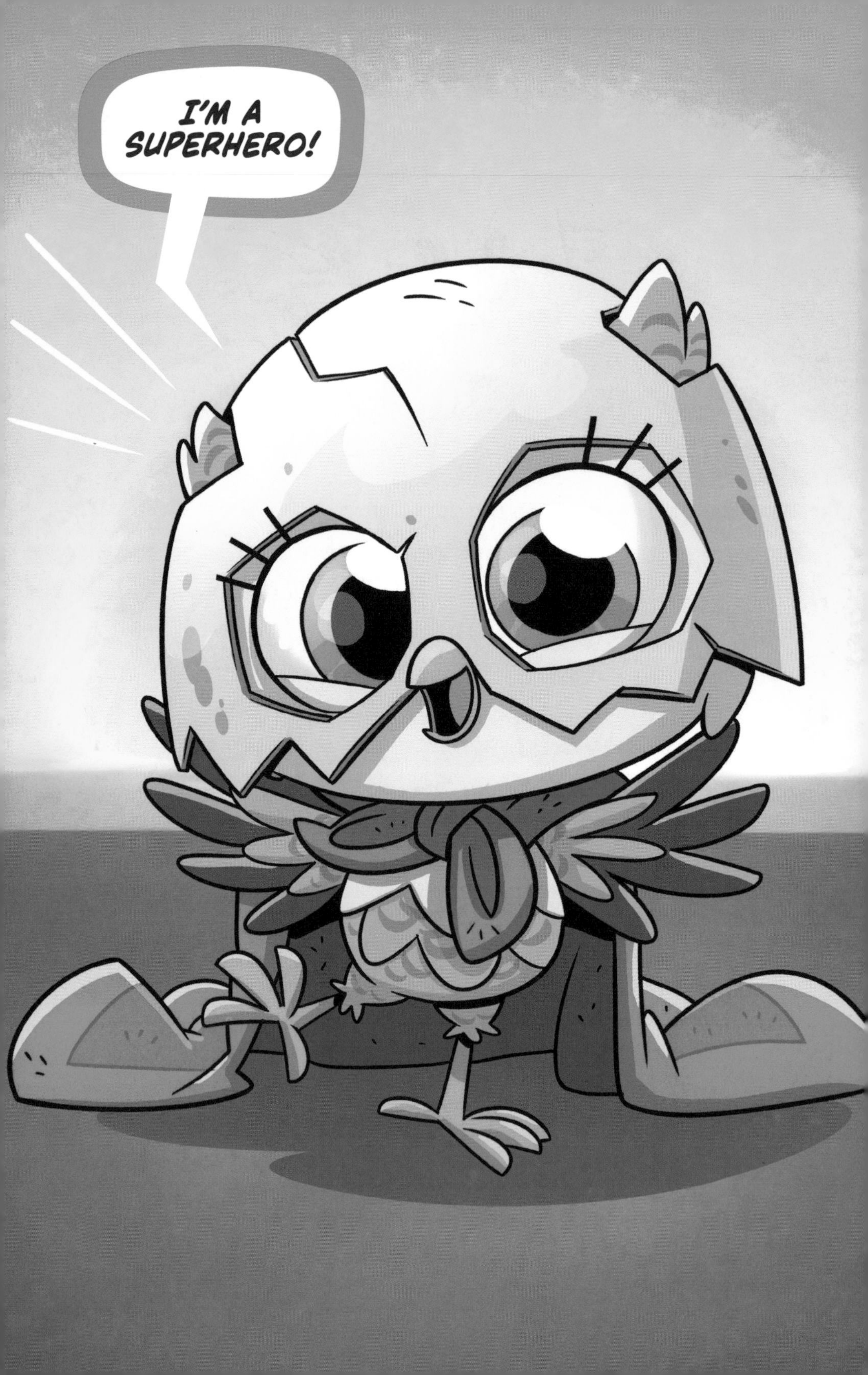
I'M A SUPERHERO!

Chapter 3: *Time Heist*

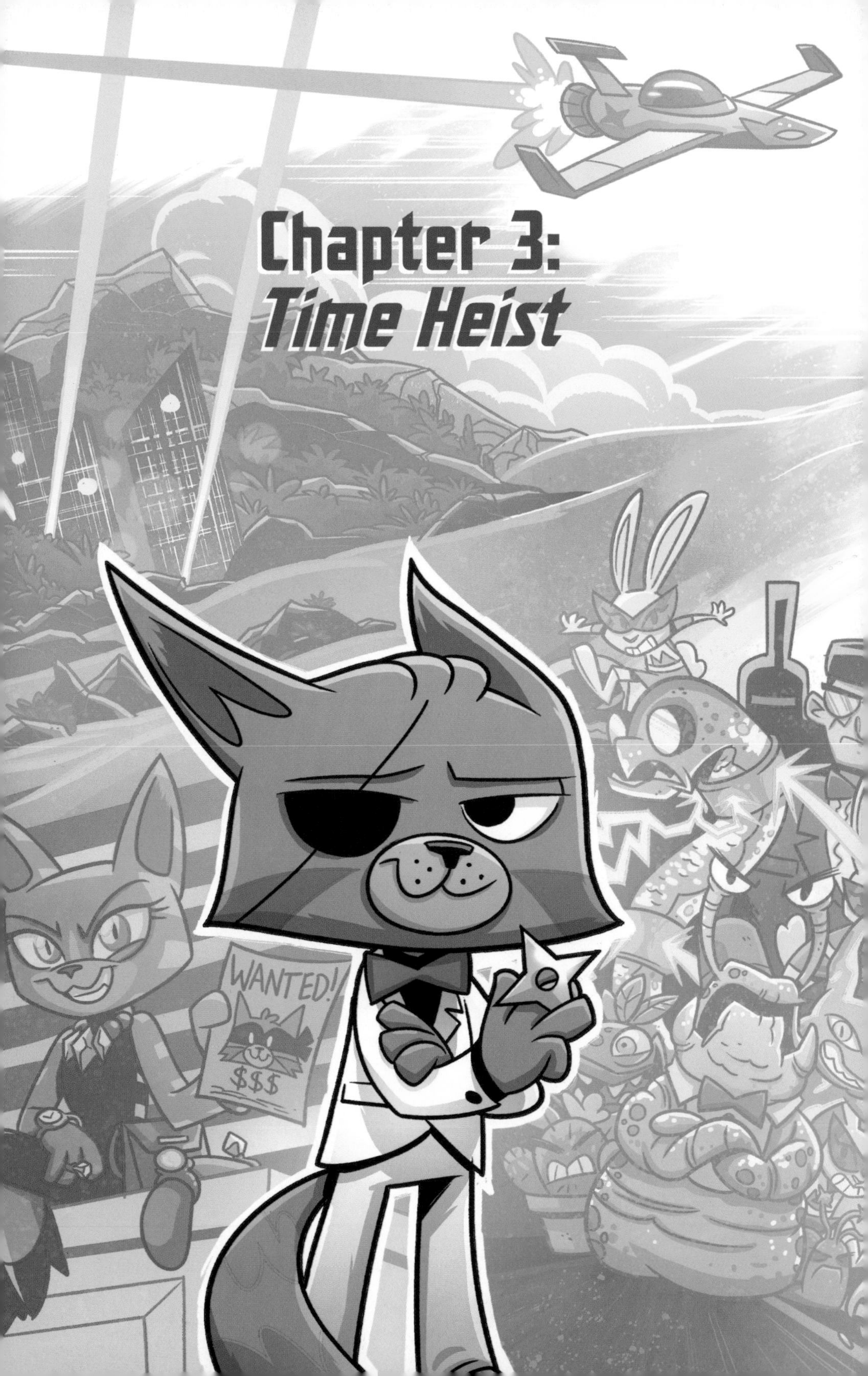
WANTED!
$$$

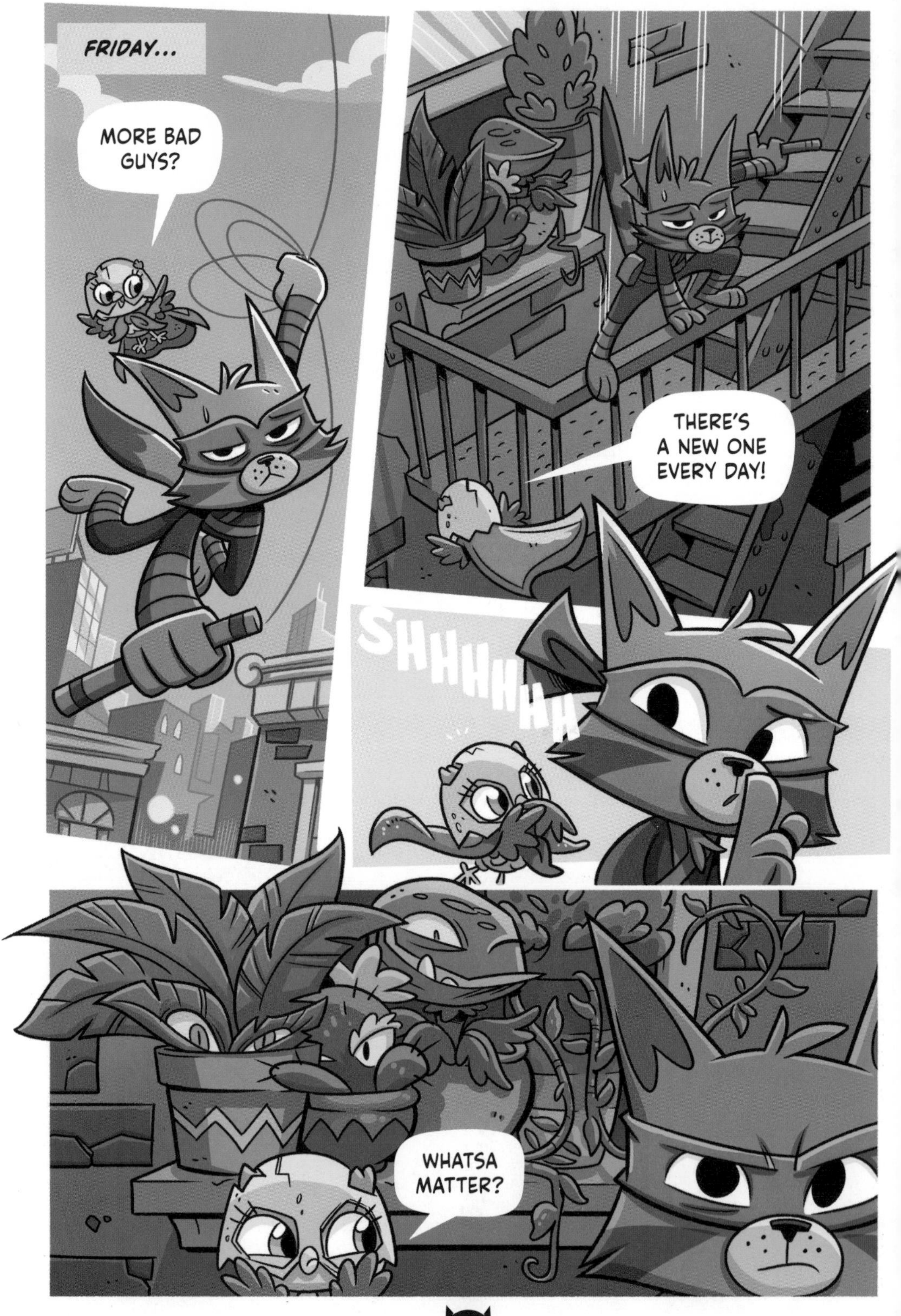
FRIDAY...
MORE BAD GUYS?
THERE'S A NEW ONE EVERY DAY!
SHHHHHHH
WHATSA MATTER?

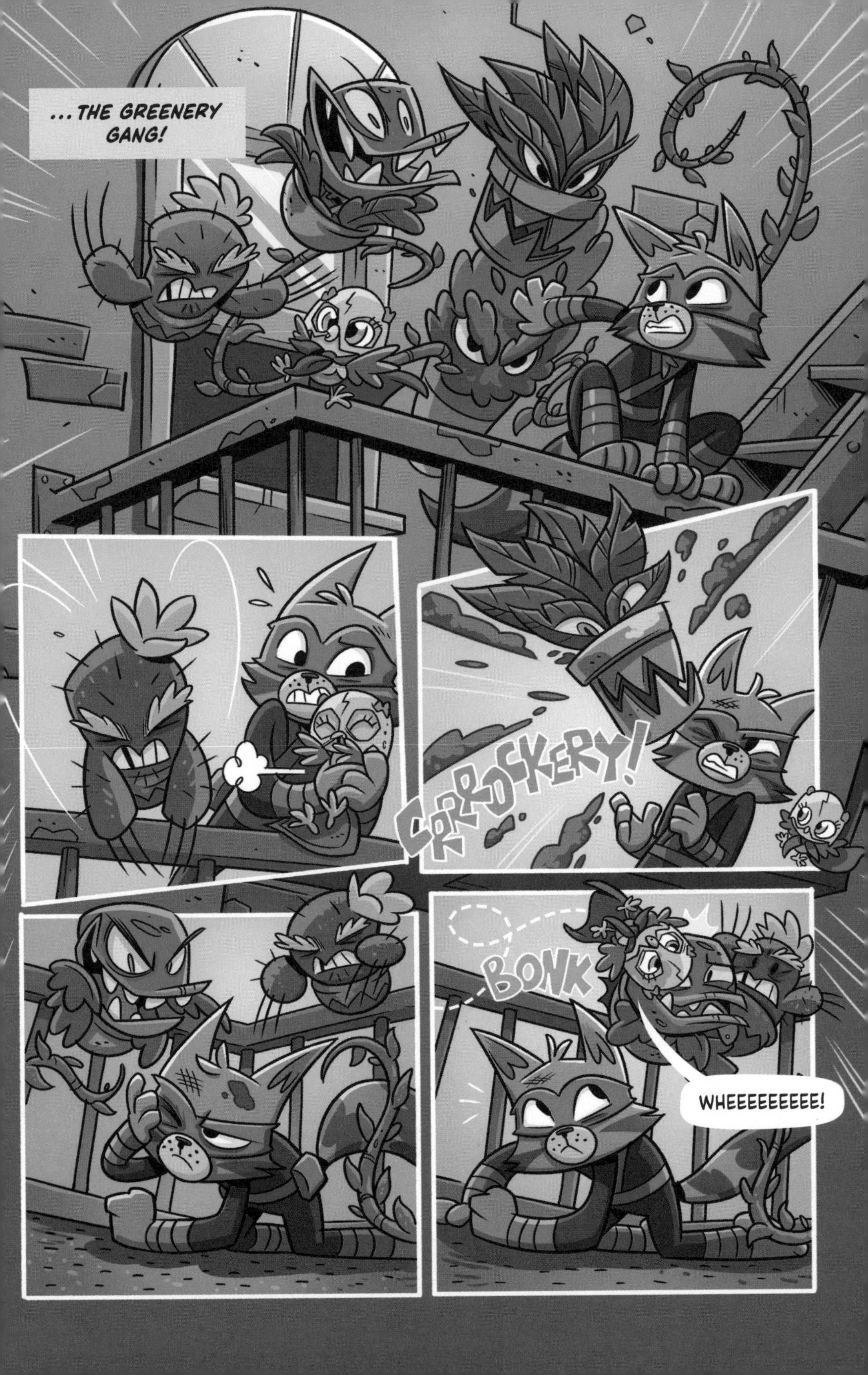
...THE GREENERY GANG!
CRRROCKERY!
BONK
WHEEEEEEEEE!

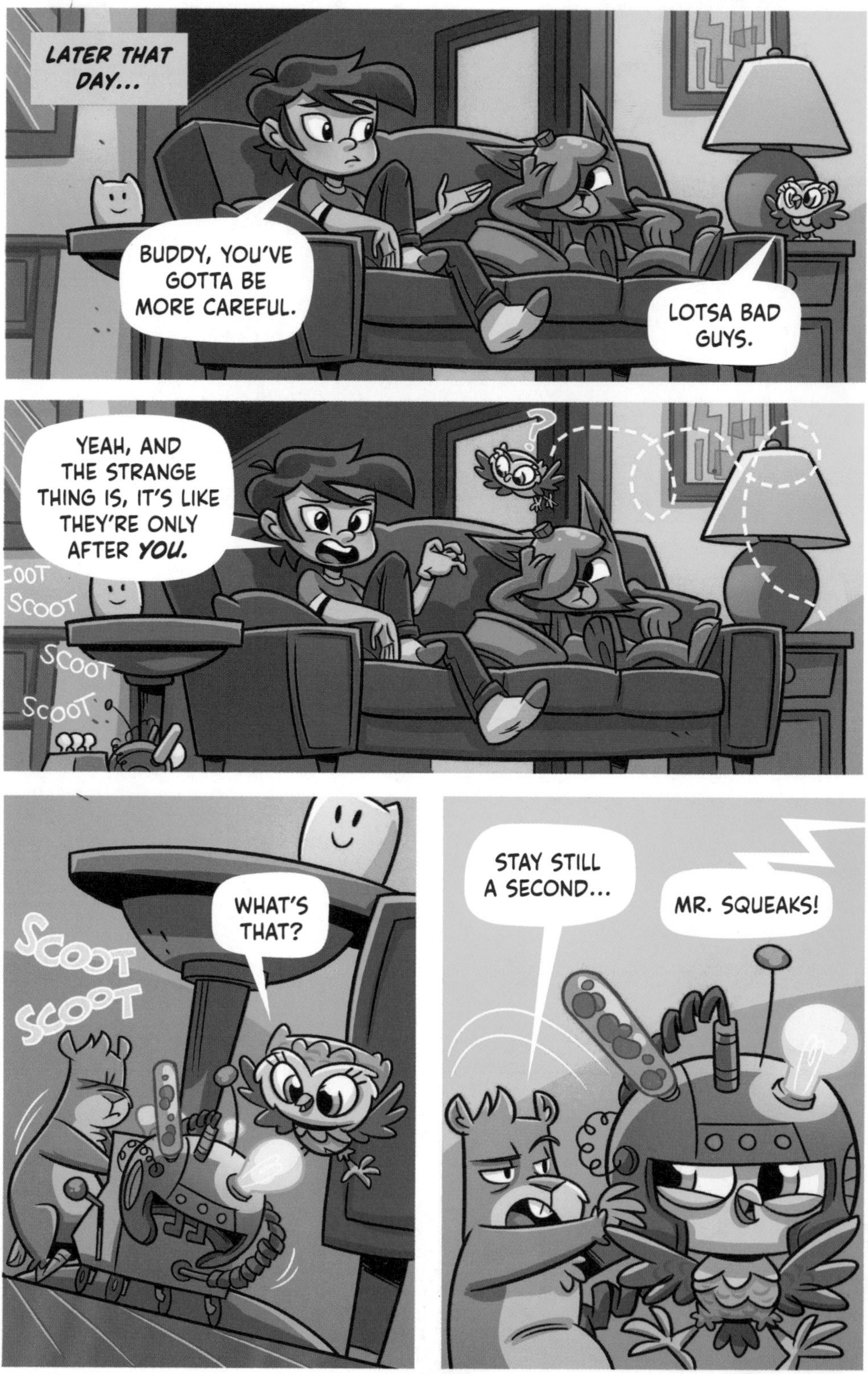
LATER THAT DAY...
BUDDY, YOU'VE GOTTA BE MORE CAREFUL.
LOTSA BAD GUYS.
YEAH, AND THE STRANGE THING IS, IT'S LIKE THEY'RE ONLY AFTER *YOU.*
SCOOT SCOOT
SCOOT
SCOOT
?
SCOOT
SCOOT
WHAT'S THAT?
STAY STILL A SECOND...
MR. SQUEAKS!

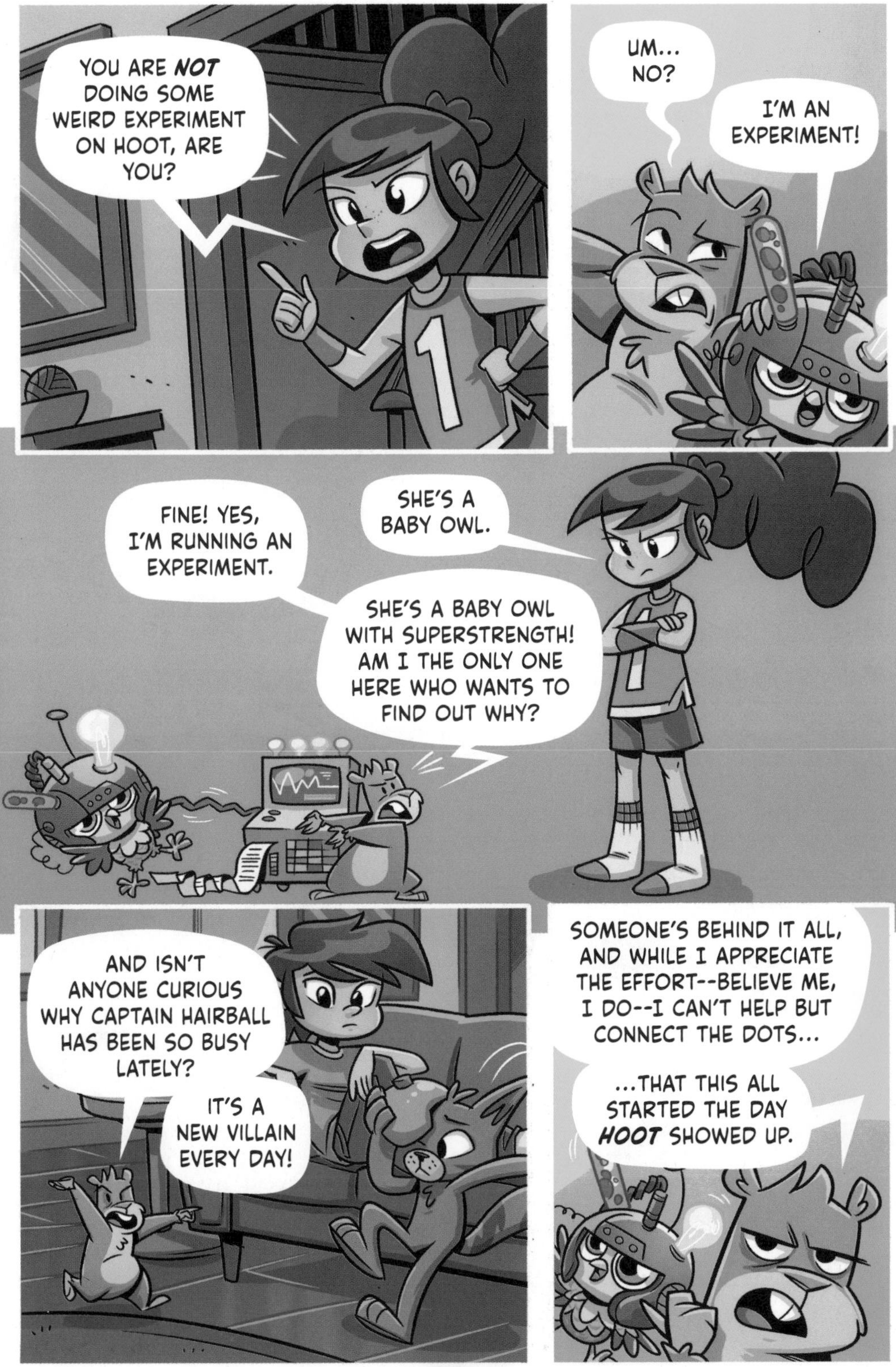

YOU ARE ***NOT*** DOING SOME WEIRD EXPERIMENT ON HOOT, ARE YOU?
UM... NO?
I'M AN EXPERIMENT!
FINE! YES, I'M RUNNING AN EXPERIMENT.
SHE'S A BABY OWL.
SHE'S A BABY OWL WITH SUPERSTRENGTH! AM I THE ONLY ONE HERE WHO WANTS TO FIND OUT WHY?
AND ISN'T ANYONE CURIOUS WHY CAPTAIN HAIRBALL HAS BEEN SO BUSY LATELY?
IT'S A NEW VILLAIN EVERY DAY!
SOMEONE'S BEHIND IT ALL, AND WHILE I APPRECIATE THE EFFORT--BELIEVE ME, I DO--I CAN'T HELP BUT CONNECT THE DOTS...
...THAT THIS ALL STARTED THE DAY ***HOOT*** SHOWED UP.

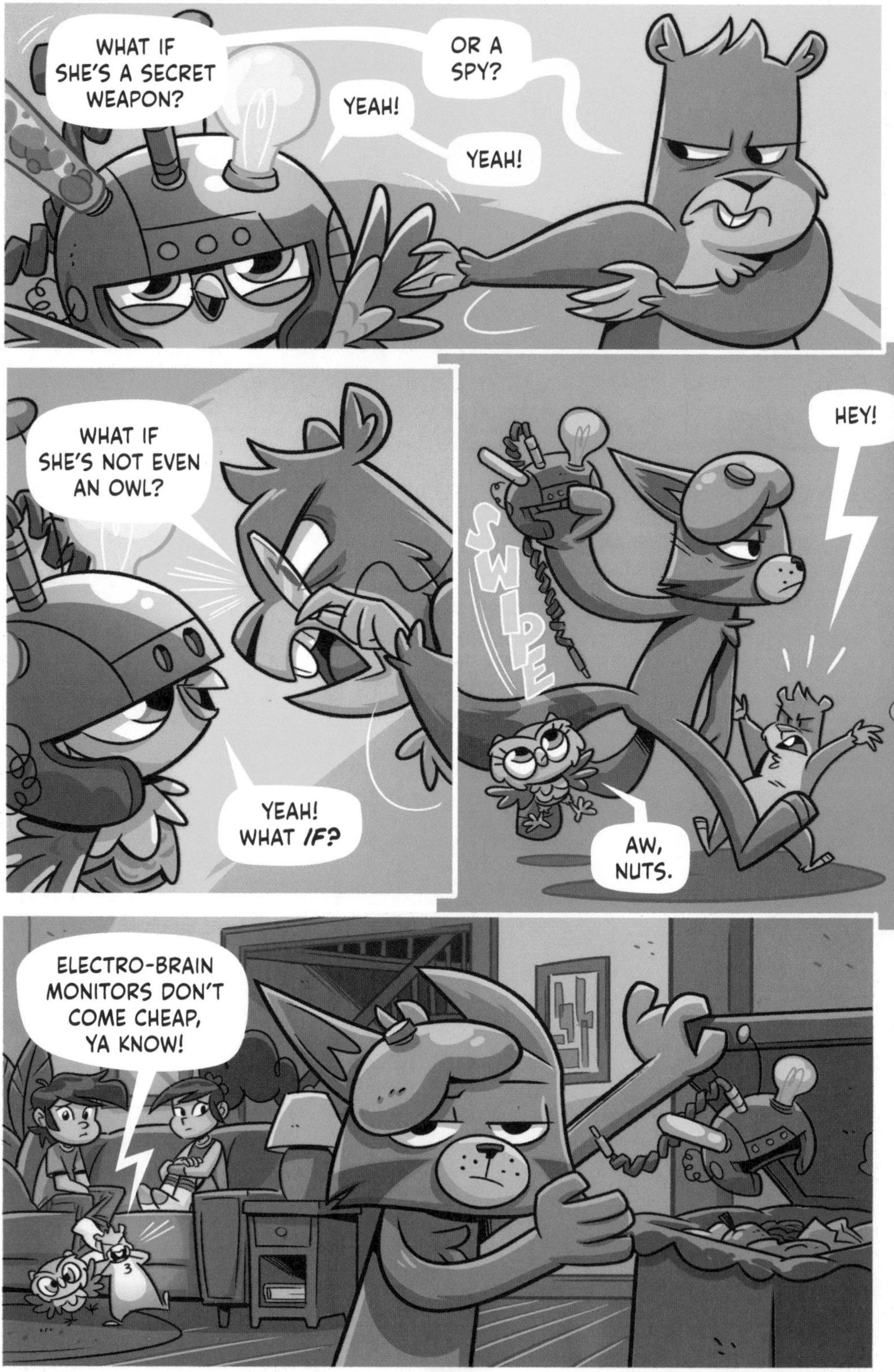
WHAT IF SHE'S A SECRET WEAPON?
OR A SPY?
YEAH!
YEAH!
WHAT IF SHE'S NOT EVEN AN OWL?
YEAH! WHAT IF?
HEY!
SWIPE
AW, NUTS.
ELECTRO-BRAIN MONITORS DON'T COME CHEAP, YA KNOW!

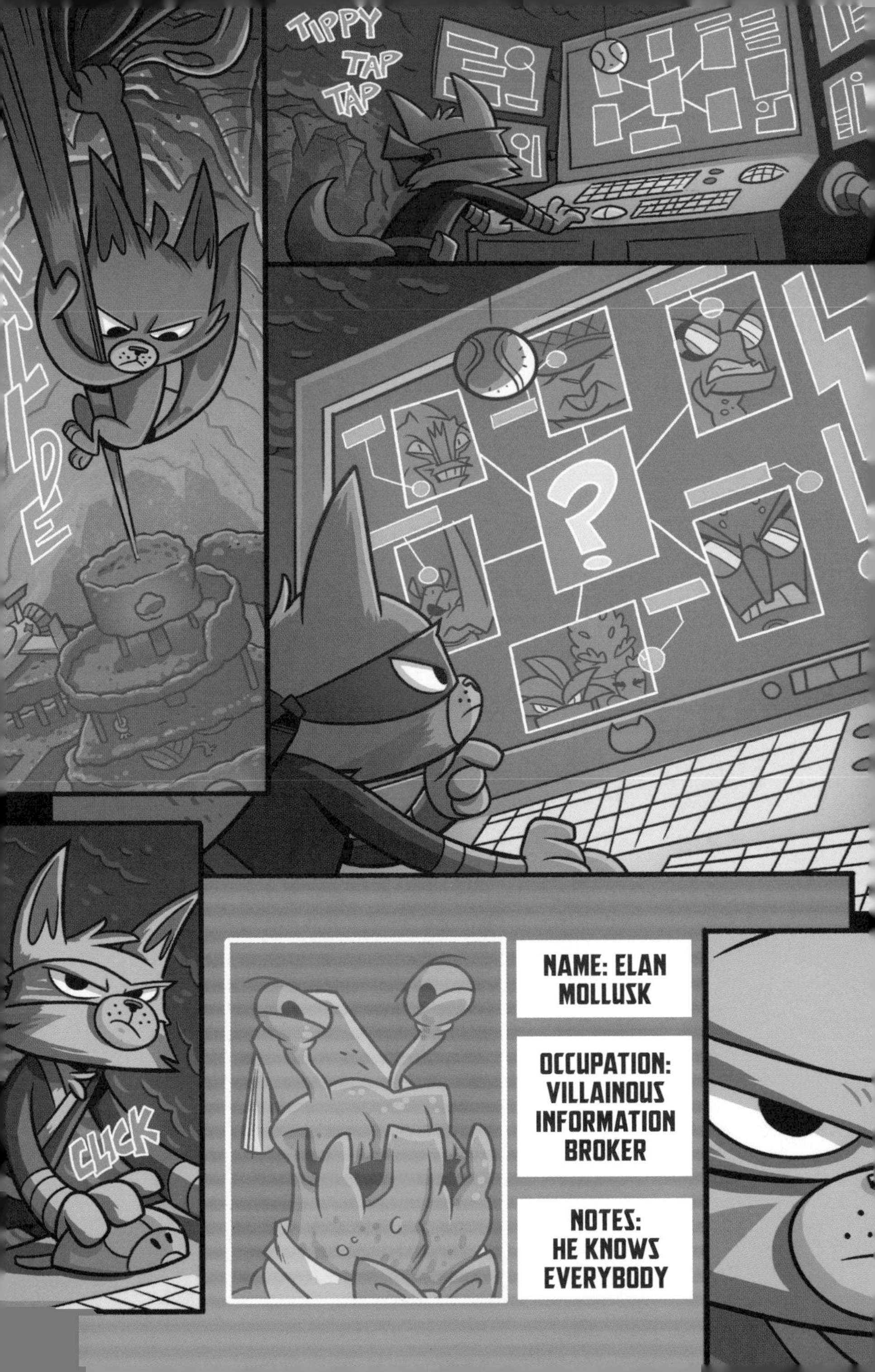
SLIDE
TIPPY
TAP
TAP
CLICK
NAME: ELAN MOLLUSK
OCCUPATION: VILLAINOUS INFORMATION BROKER
NOTES: HE KNOWS EVERYBODY

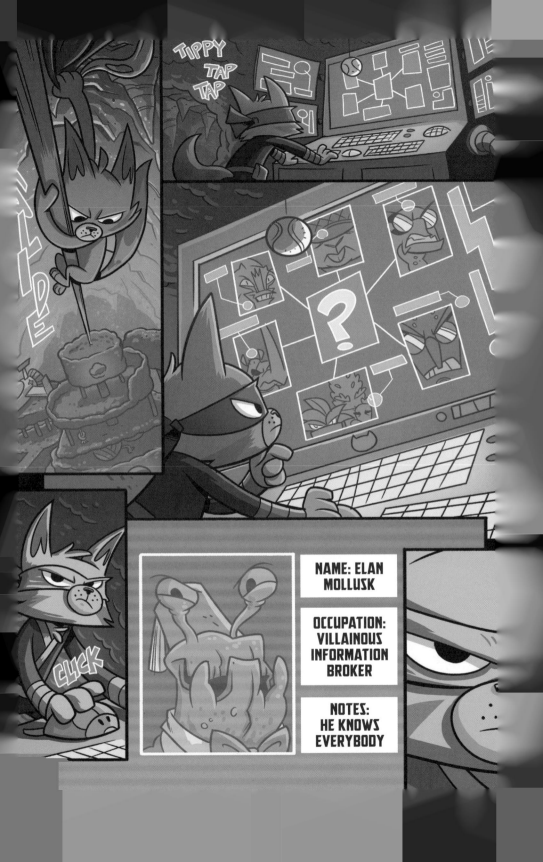

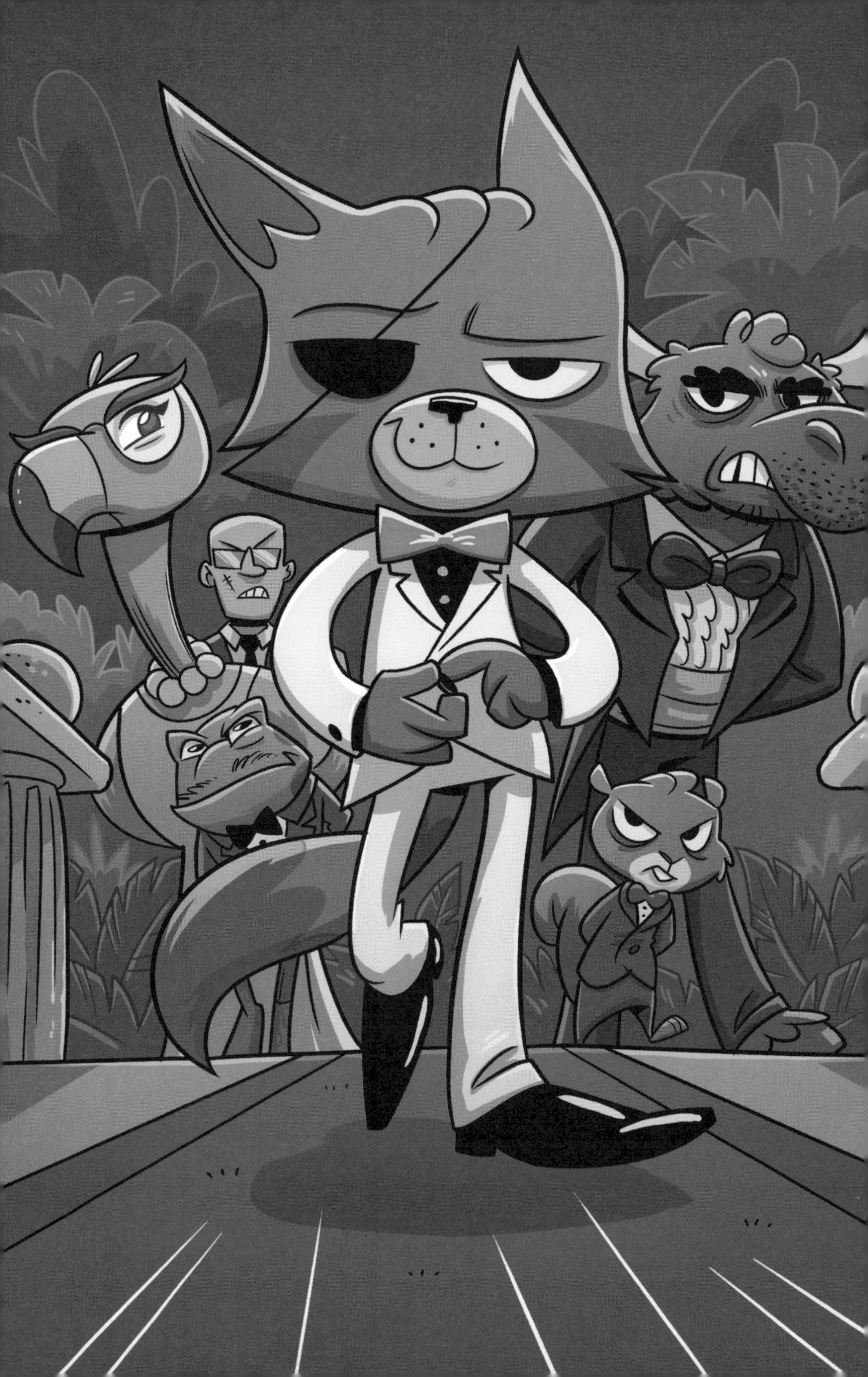

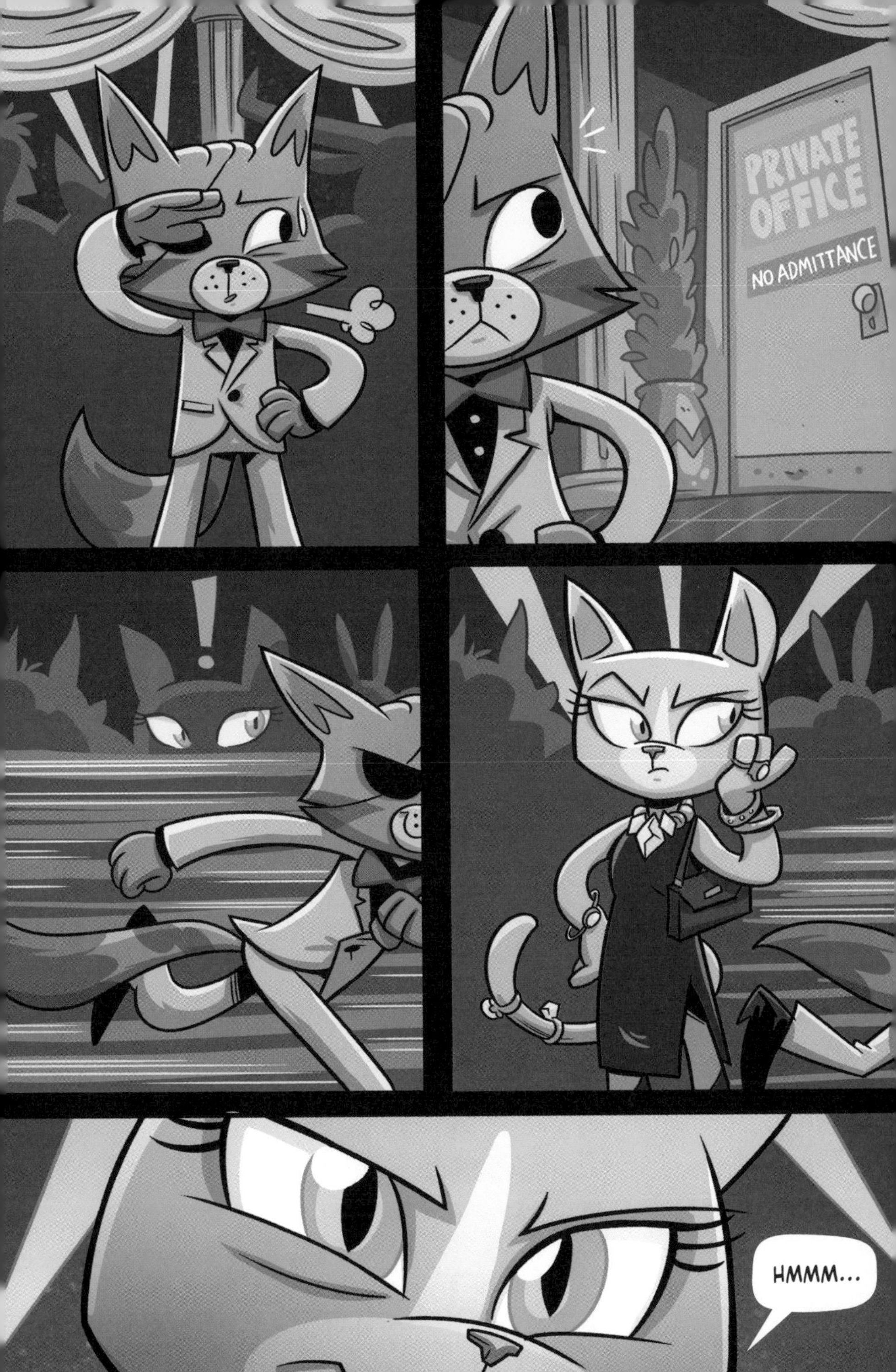
PRIVATE OFFICE
NO ADMITTANCE
!
HMMM...

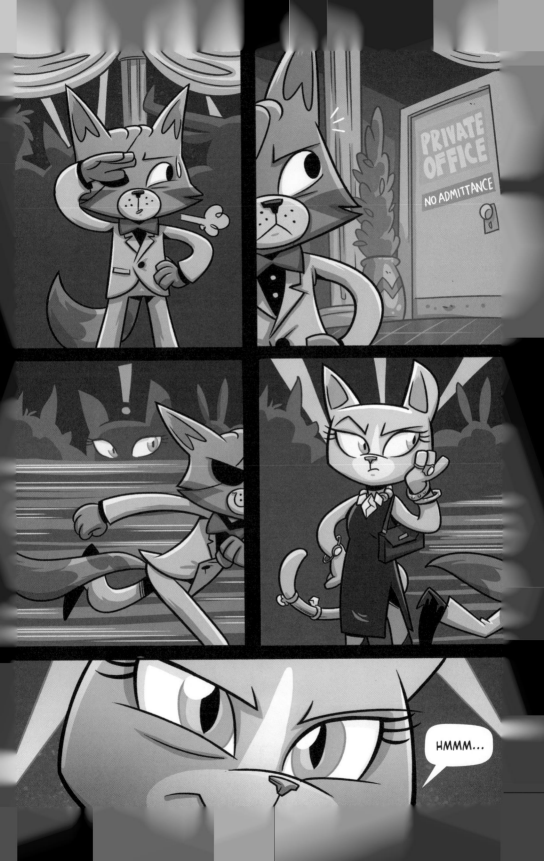

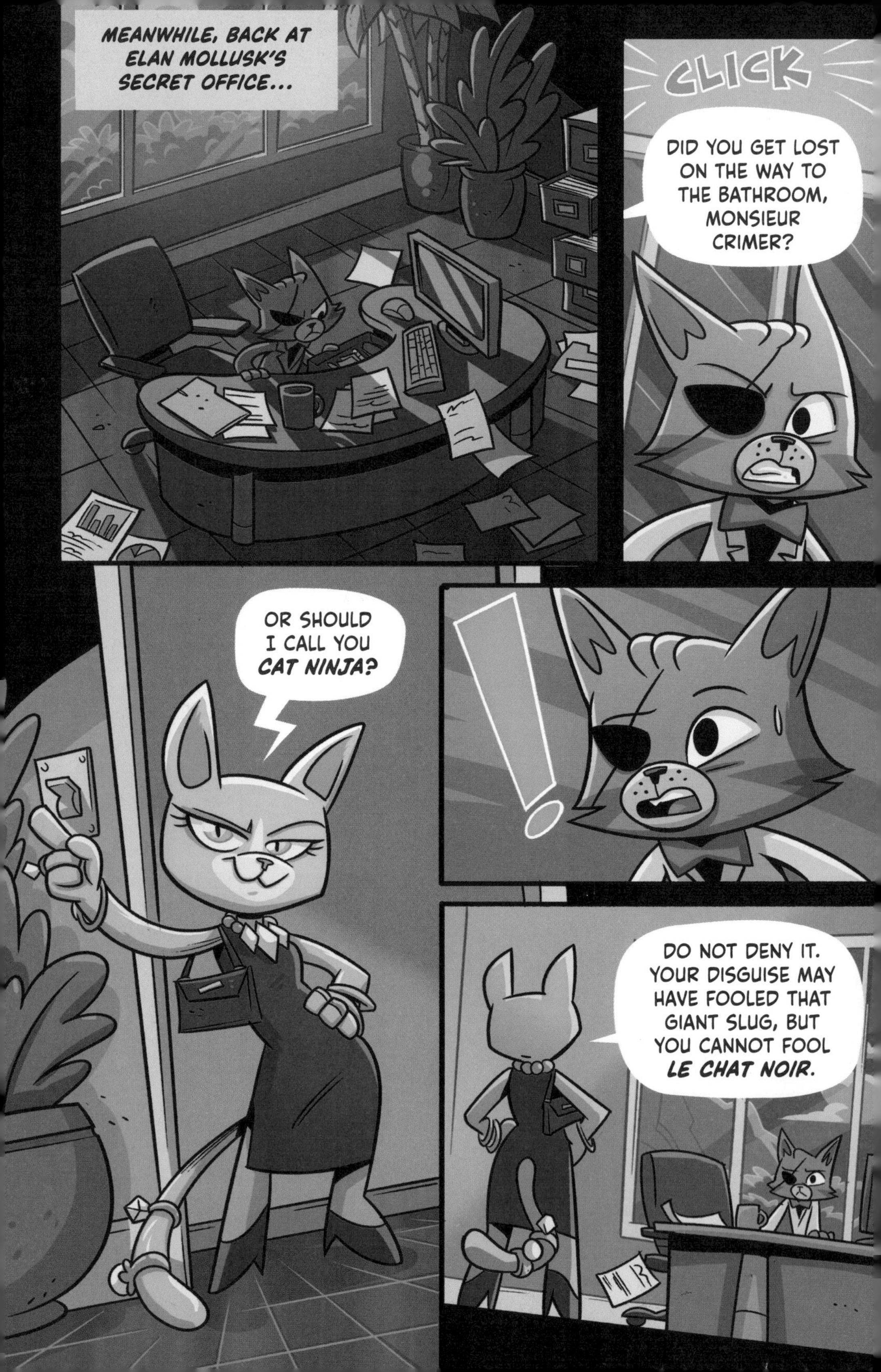
MEANWHILE, BACK AT ELAN MOLLUSK'S SECRET OFFICE...
CLICK
DID YOU GET LOST ON THE WAY TO THE BATHROOM, MONSIEUR CRIMER?
OR SHOULD I CALL YOU *CAT NINJA?*
!
DO NOT DENY IT. YOUR DISGUISE MAY HAVE FOOLED THAT GIANT SLUG, BUT YOU CANNOT FOOL *LE CHAT NOIR.*

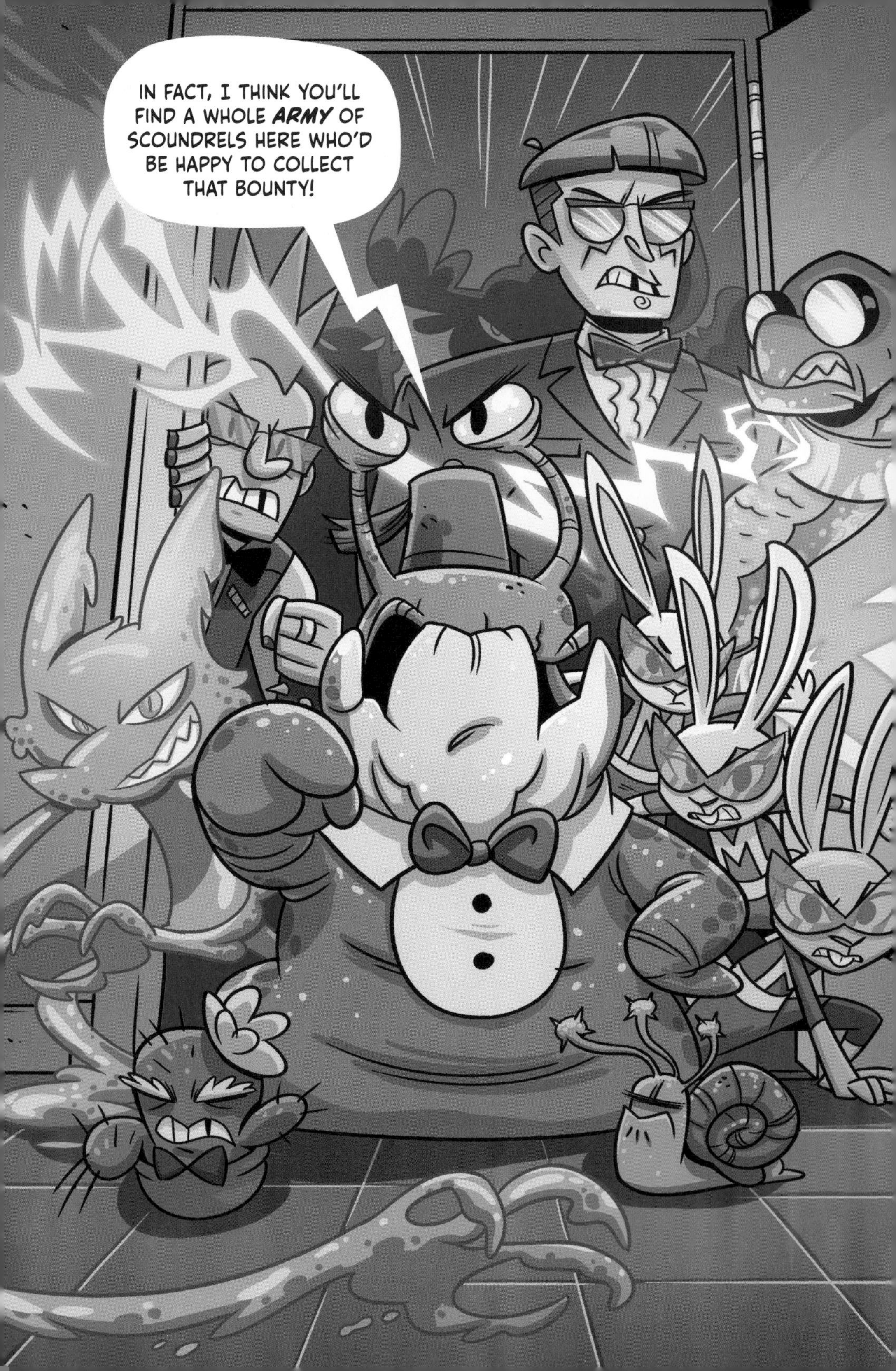
IN FACT, I THINK YOU'LL FIND A WHOLE *ARMY* OF SCOUNDRELS HERE WHO'D BE HAPPY TO COLLECT THAT BOUNTY!

Chapter 4: *Night of the Cuckoo*

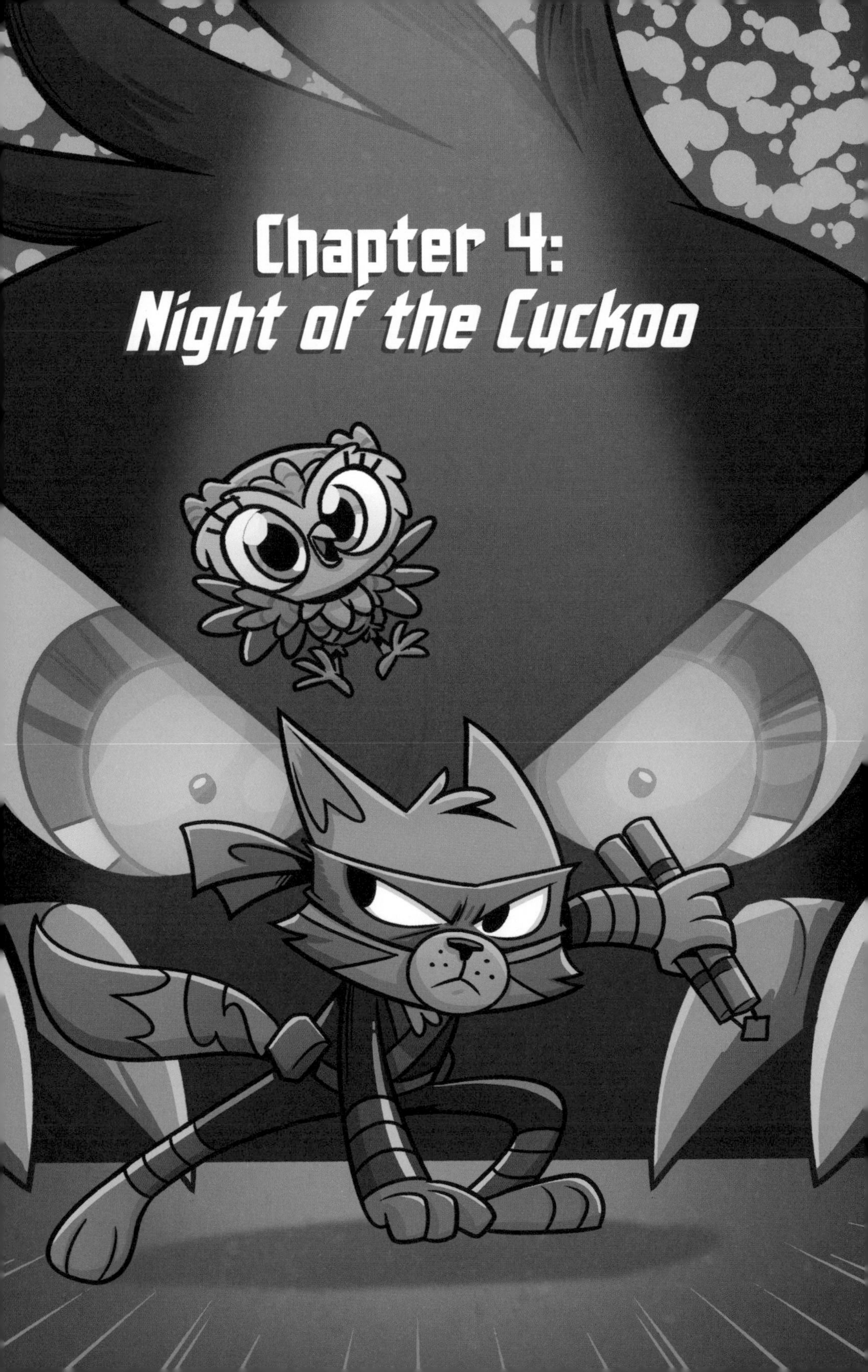

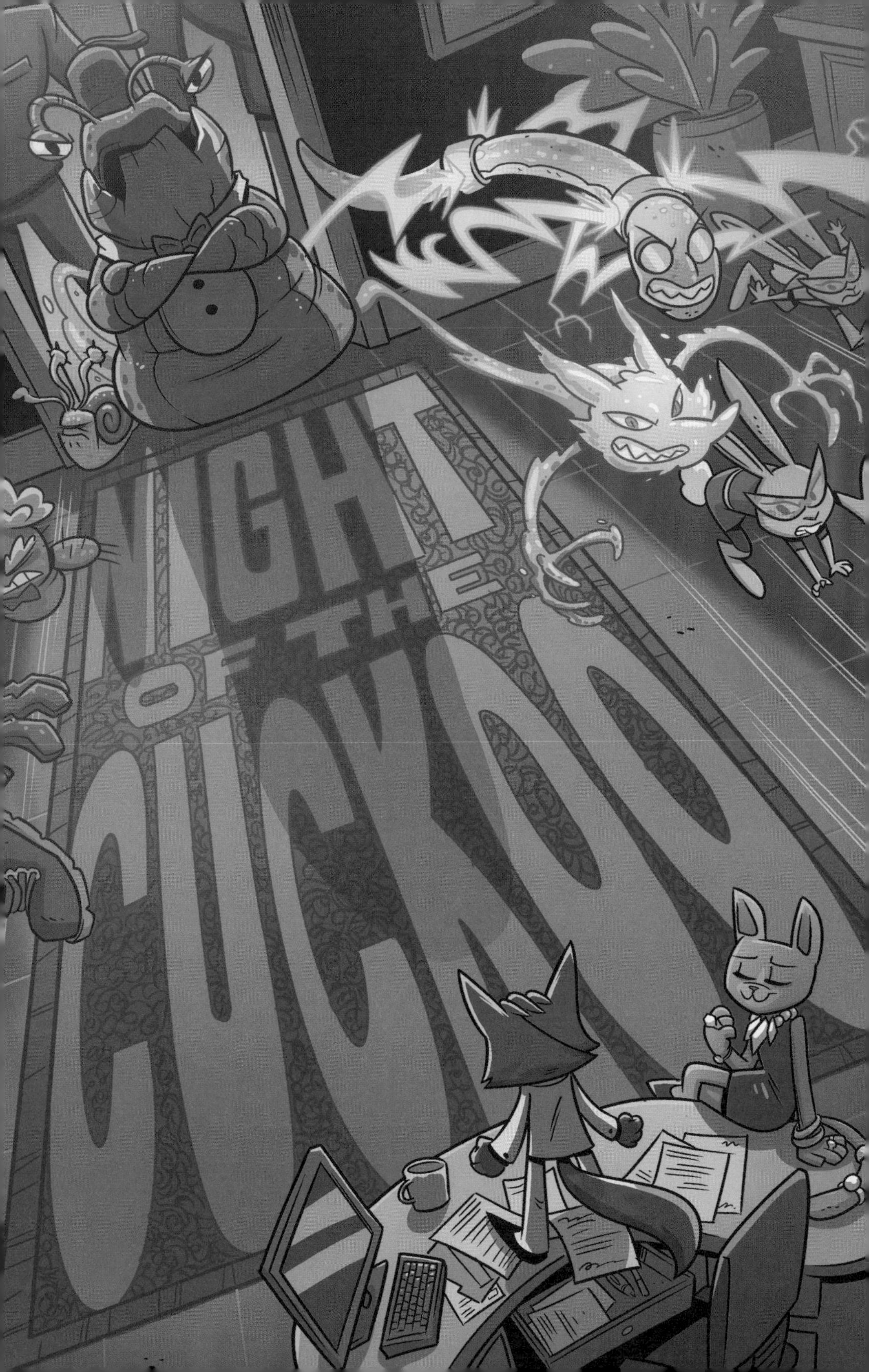
NIGHT OF THE CUCKOO

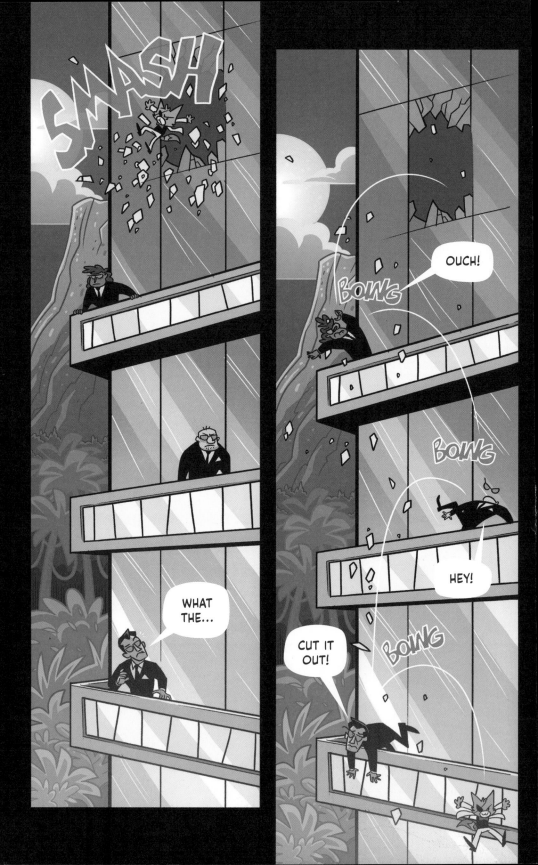

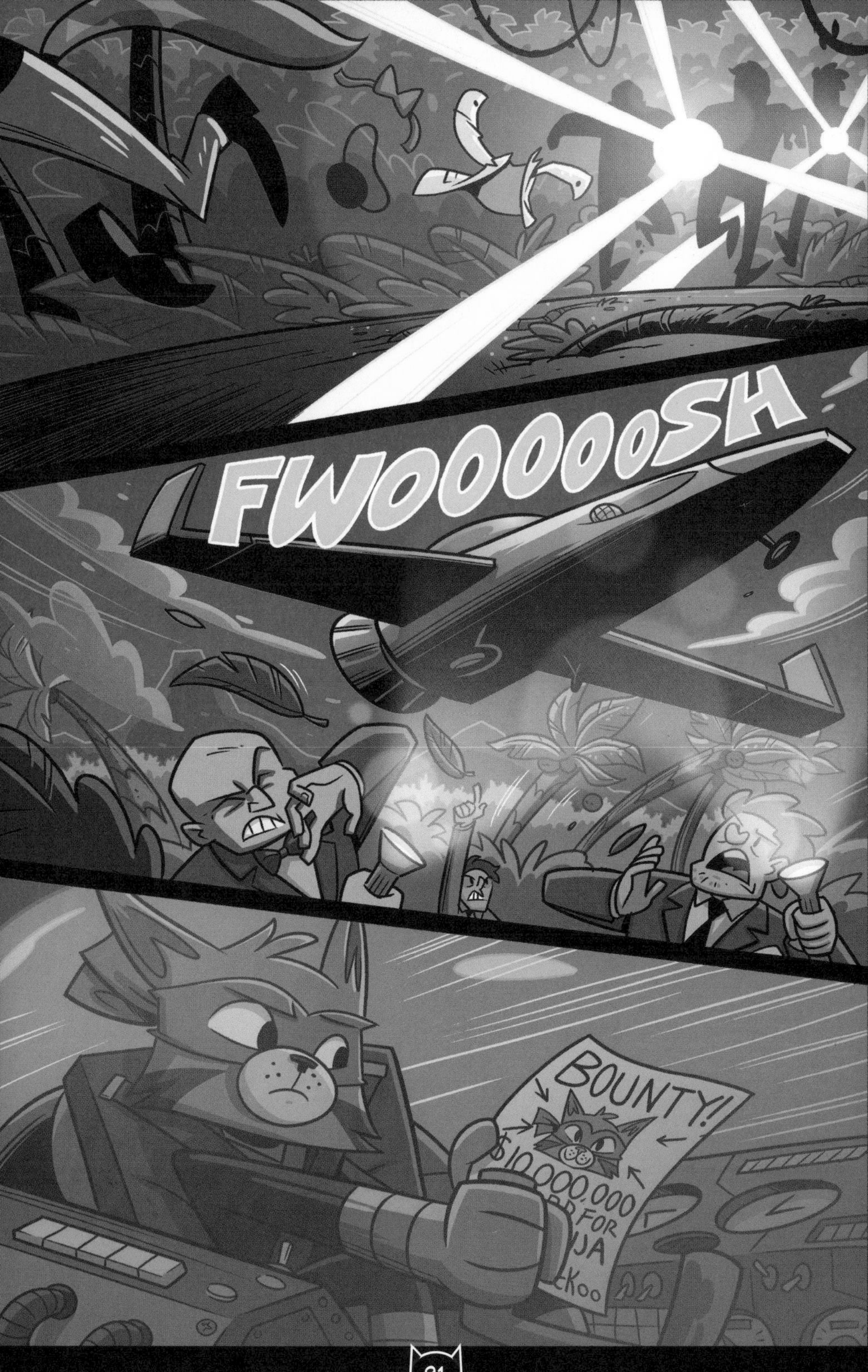
FWOOOOOOSH
BOUNTY!
$10,000,000

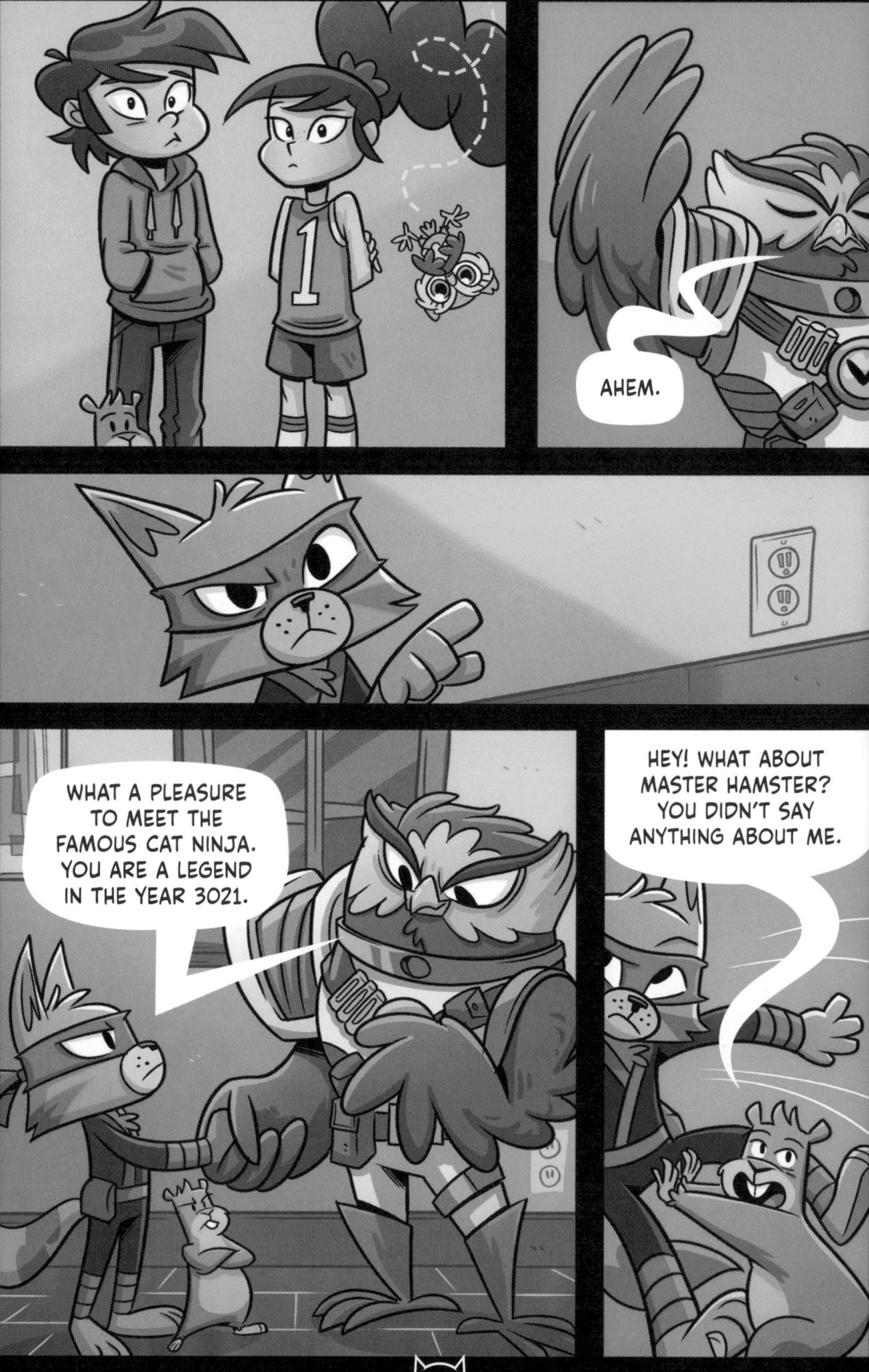
AHEM.
WHAT A PLEASURE TO MEET THE FAMOUS CAT NINJA. YOU ARE A LEGEND IN THE YEAR 3021.
HEY! WHAT ABOUT MASTER HAMSTER? YOU DIDN'T SAY ANYTHING ABOUT ME.

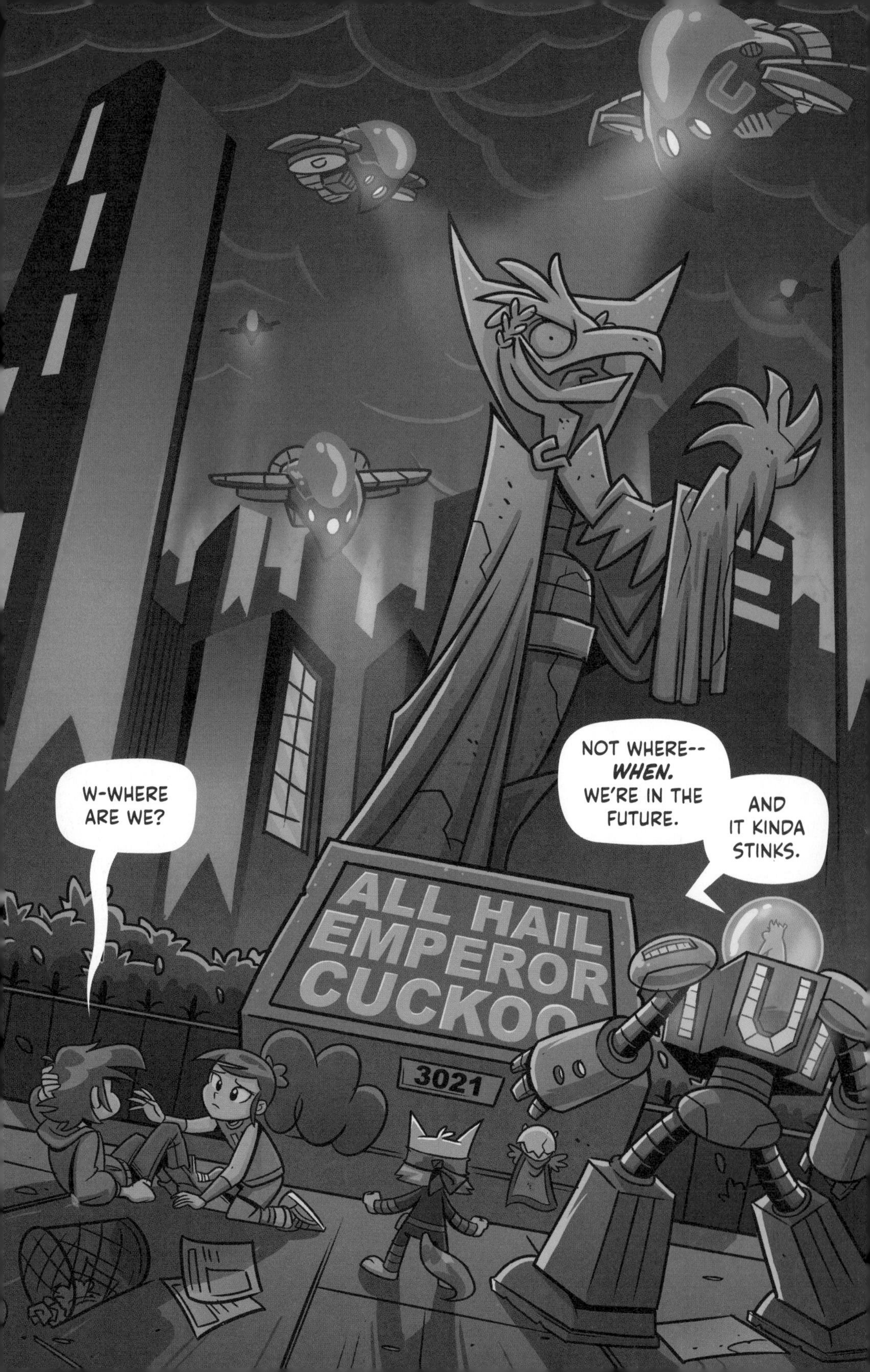

ALL HAIL EMPEROR CUCKOO
3021
W-WHERE ARE WE?
NOT WHERE-- *WHEN.* WE'RE IN THE FUTURE.
AND IT KINDA STINKS.

Chapter 5:
Escape from...the Future!

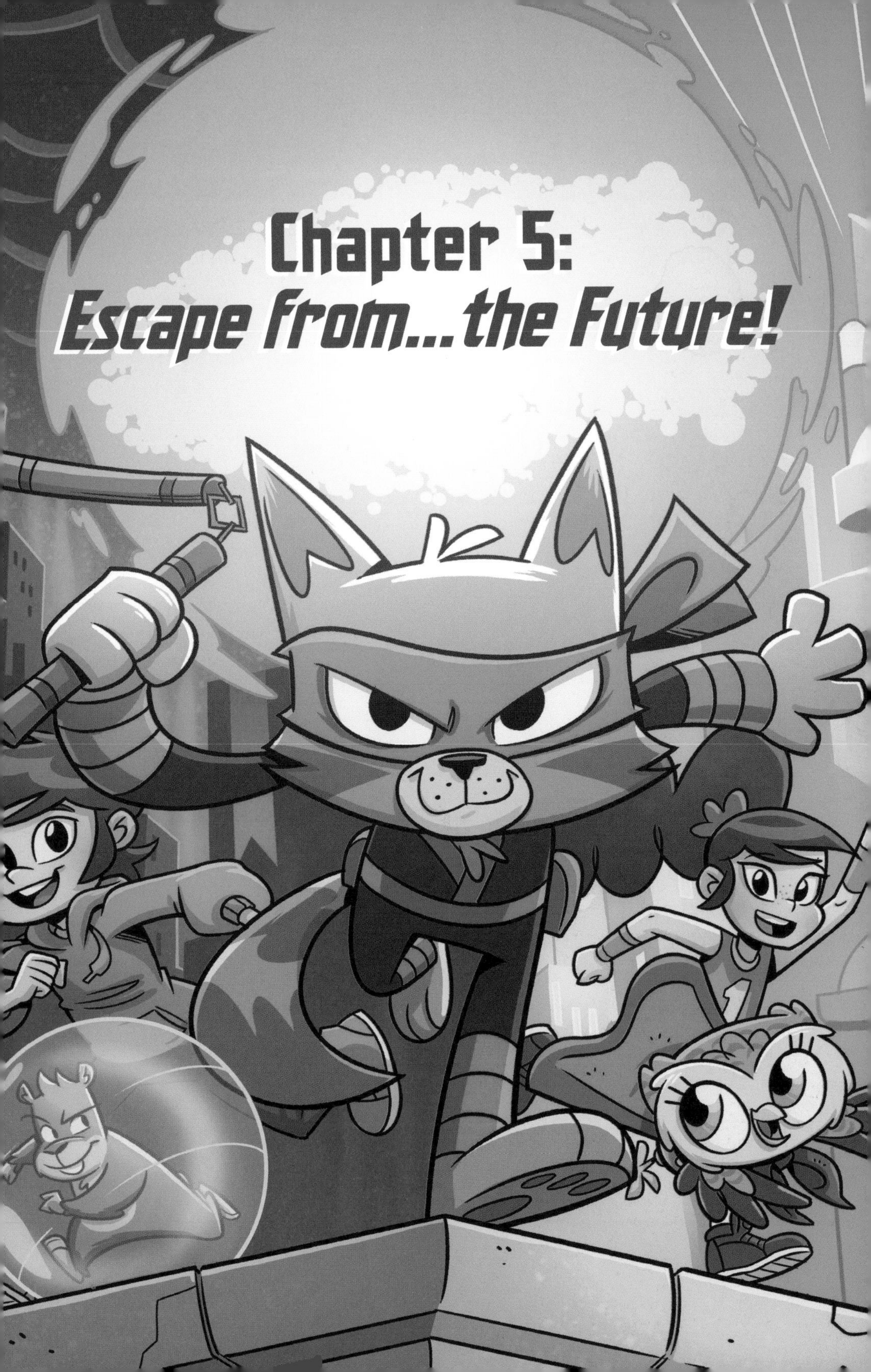

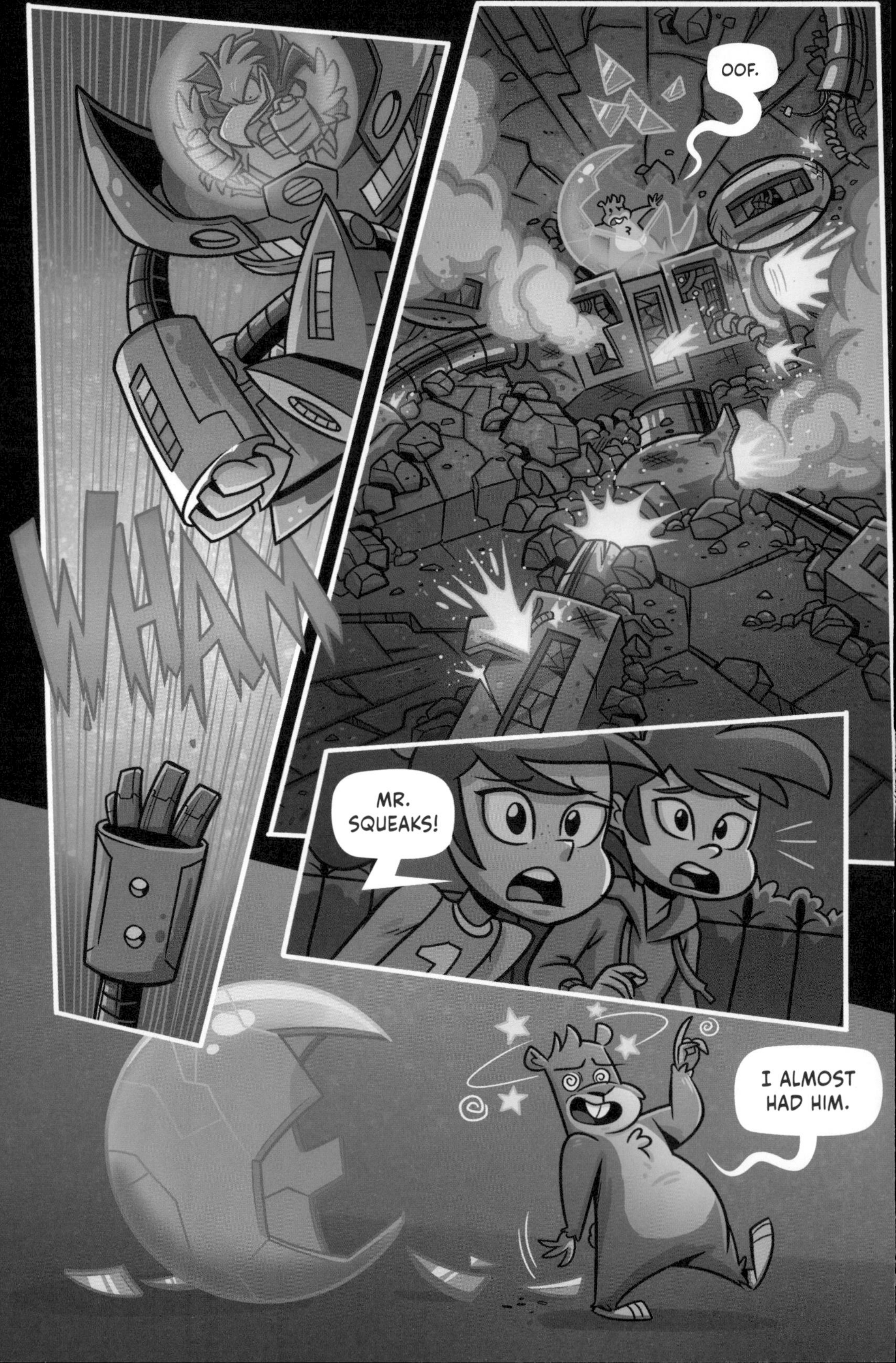
WHAM
OOF.
MR. SQUEAKS!
I ALMOST HAD HIM.

OFF ON THE MUSHY REUNION UNTIL SOMEONE EXPLAINS WHAT'S HAPPENING HERE?
IT'S ALL MY FAULT. YOU SEE, I AM...I *WAS* A TIME TRAVELER.
"EXPLORATION IS MY PASSION. I INVENTED THE TIME HARNESS SO I COULD SEE HISTORY IN ACTION!
"BUT WHENEVER I VISITED THE PAST, I WAS CAREFUL NOT TO CHANGE ANYTHING, FOR FEAR OF WHAT IT MIGHT DO TO THE FUTURE.
"THE CUCKOO SHOWED NO SUCH RESTRAINT.
FWOOM
"HE STOLE MY TIME HARNESS AND WENT BACK TO *FIX* HIS PAST. HE TURNED HIS LOSSES INTO WINS."
PSST! HERE'S THE KEY TO YOUR CELL. YOU'LL THANK ME LATER.

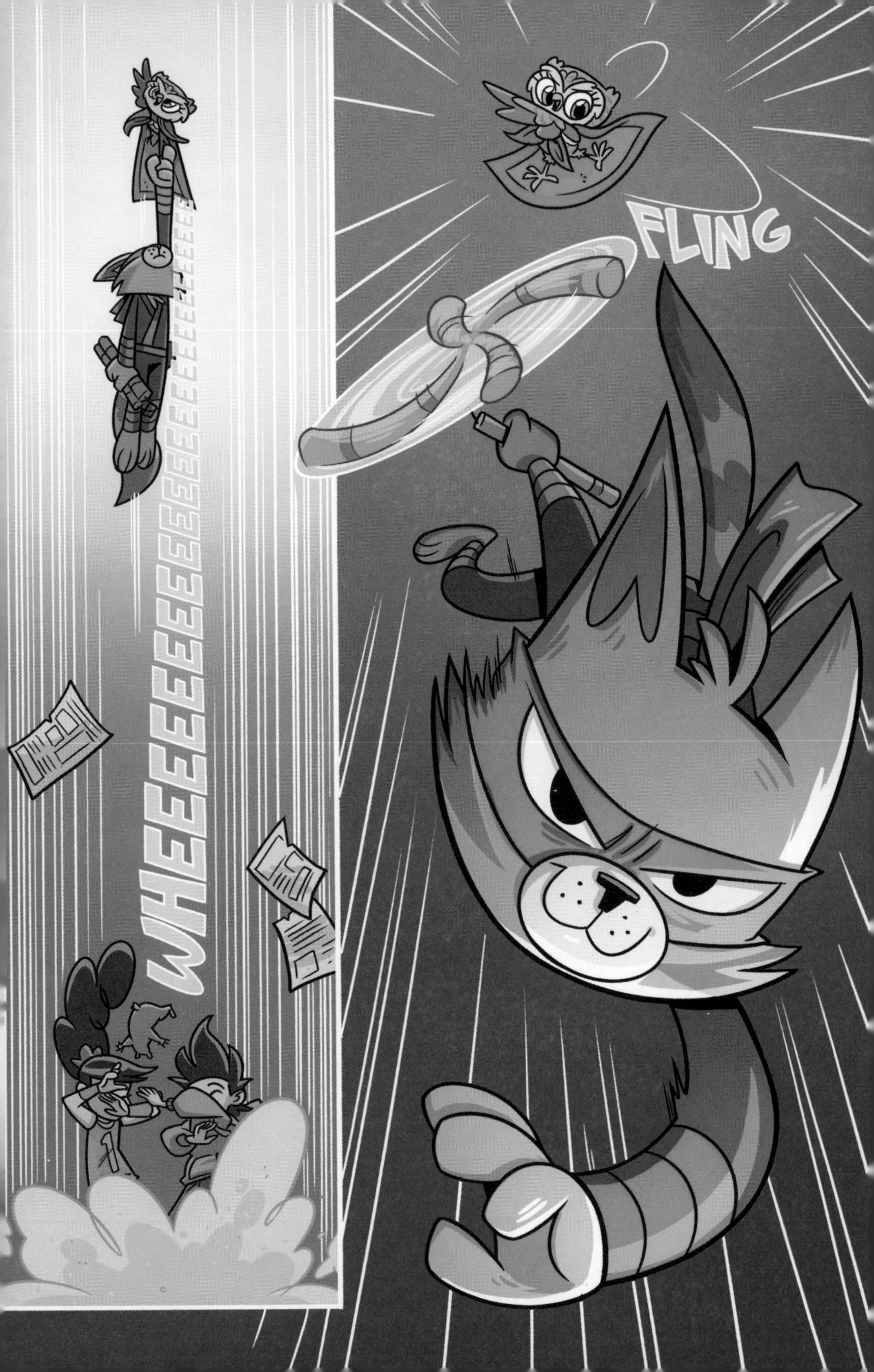
FLING
WHEEEEEEEEEEEEEEEEEEEEEEEEEEEEE

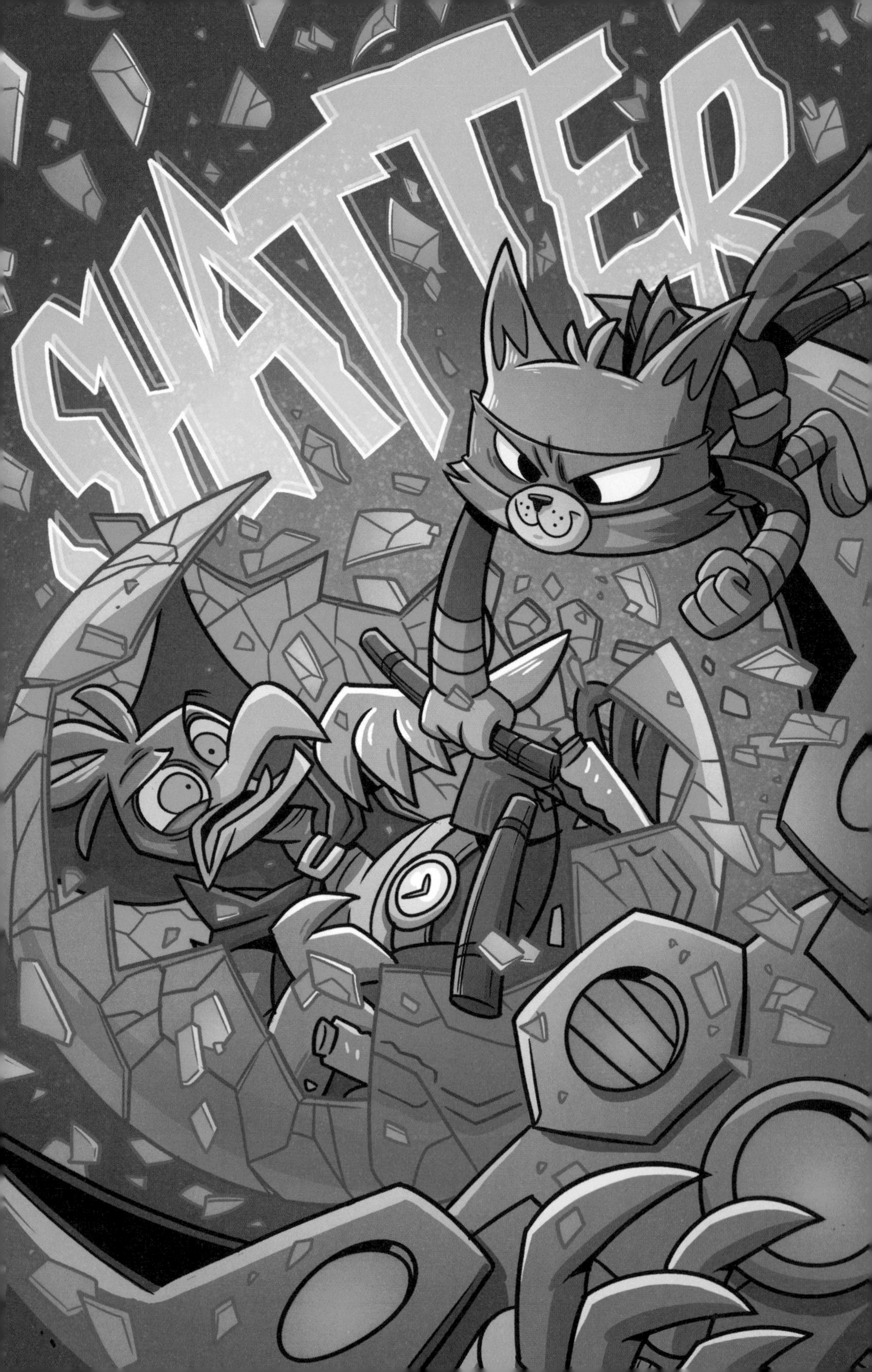
SHATTER

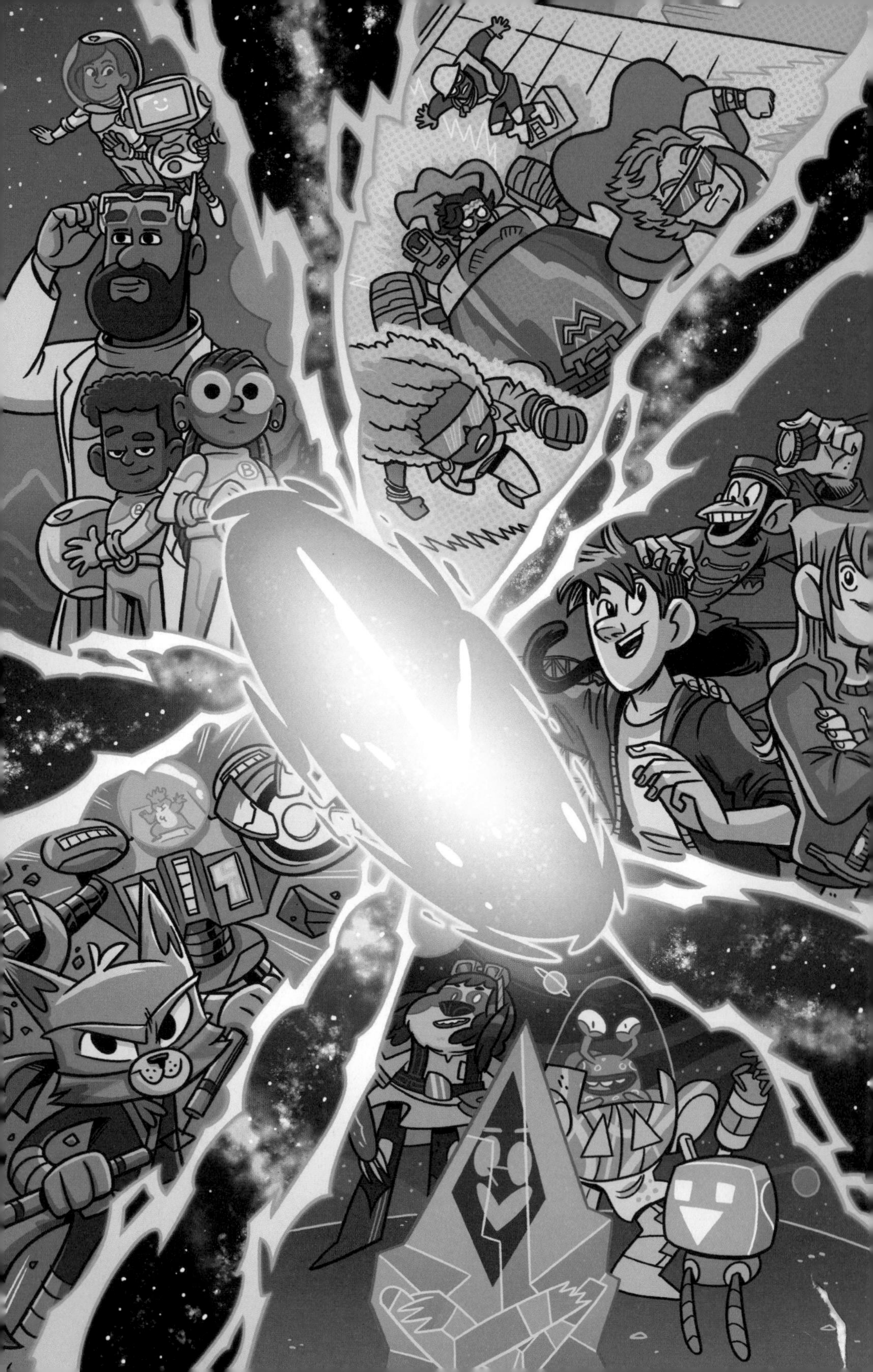

About the Author

MATTHEW CODY is the author of several popular books, including the award-winning Supers of Noble's Green trilogy: *Powerless*, *Super*, and *Villainous*. He is also the author of *Will in Scarlet* and *The Dead Gentleman*, as well as the graphic novels *Zatanna and the House of Secrets* from DC comics and *Bright Family* from Epic/Andrews McMeel. He lives in Manhattan, New York, with his wife and son.

About the Illustrator

CHAD THOMAS is an illustrator and cartoonist living with his family in McKinney, Texas. He's worked on books such as *TMNT*, *Star Wars Adventures*, and *Mega Man* and also illustrates activity and educational books. He loves his family, comic books, and Star Wars and will let his children beat him in checkers, but never in *Mario Kart*.

About the Colorist

WARREN WUCINICH is a comic book creator and part-time carny who has been lucky enough to work on such cool projects as *Invader ZIM*, *Courtney Crumrin*, and *Cat Ninja*. He is also the cocreator of the YA graphic novel *Kriss: The Gift of Wrath*. He currently resides in Dallas, Texas, where he spends his time making comics, rewatching '80s television shows, and eating all the tacos.

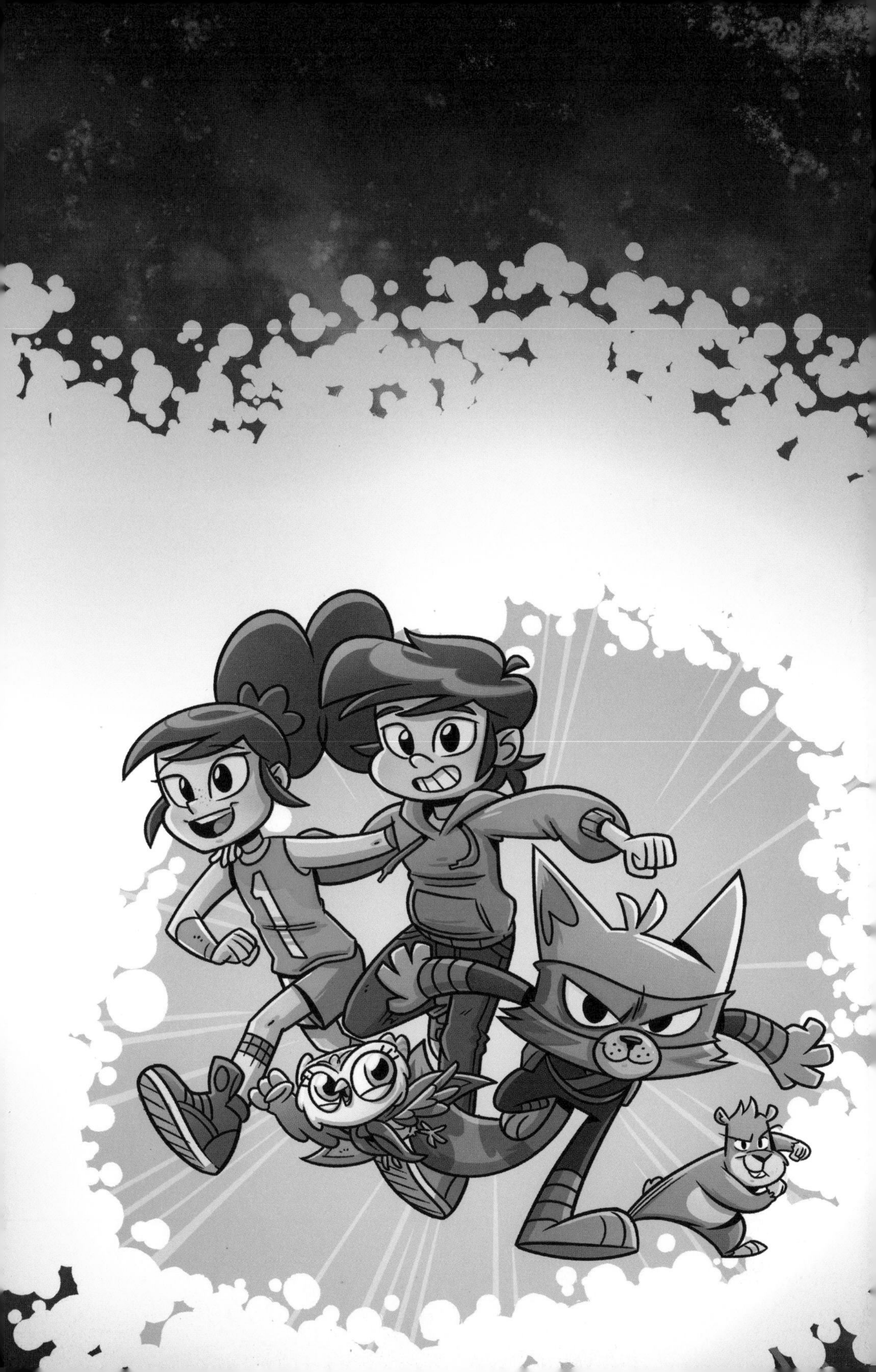

THE
ELECTRIC
EEL!

MAD SCIENTIST GOGGLES!

DID YOU KNOW
ELECTRIC EELS
ARE ACTUALLY
FISH?!

COLLARS
COLLECT HIS
ELECTRICITY
INTO ARMS
+ LEGS!

THE
CUCKOO

(WELL MAYBE
MORE OF A
VULTURE)

CRAZY
EYES!

CRACKED
TIME DEVICE

SLICK
FOX

MADE OF
OIL OR
GREASE?

A REAL
SLIMEY
CHARACTER

CAN STRETCH
AND MOVE LIKE
LIQUID

THE
ORIGINAL

DUPLICATES (BUT SHE CAN
MAKE WAY MORE)

MULTI
BUNNY

SHE CAN
DUPLICATE
HERSELF
OVER
AND OVER

A ONE-
RABBIT
TEAM

MASTER
THIEF?

MAYBE SHE'S
A RIVAL TO
LE CHAT?

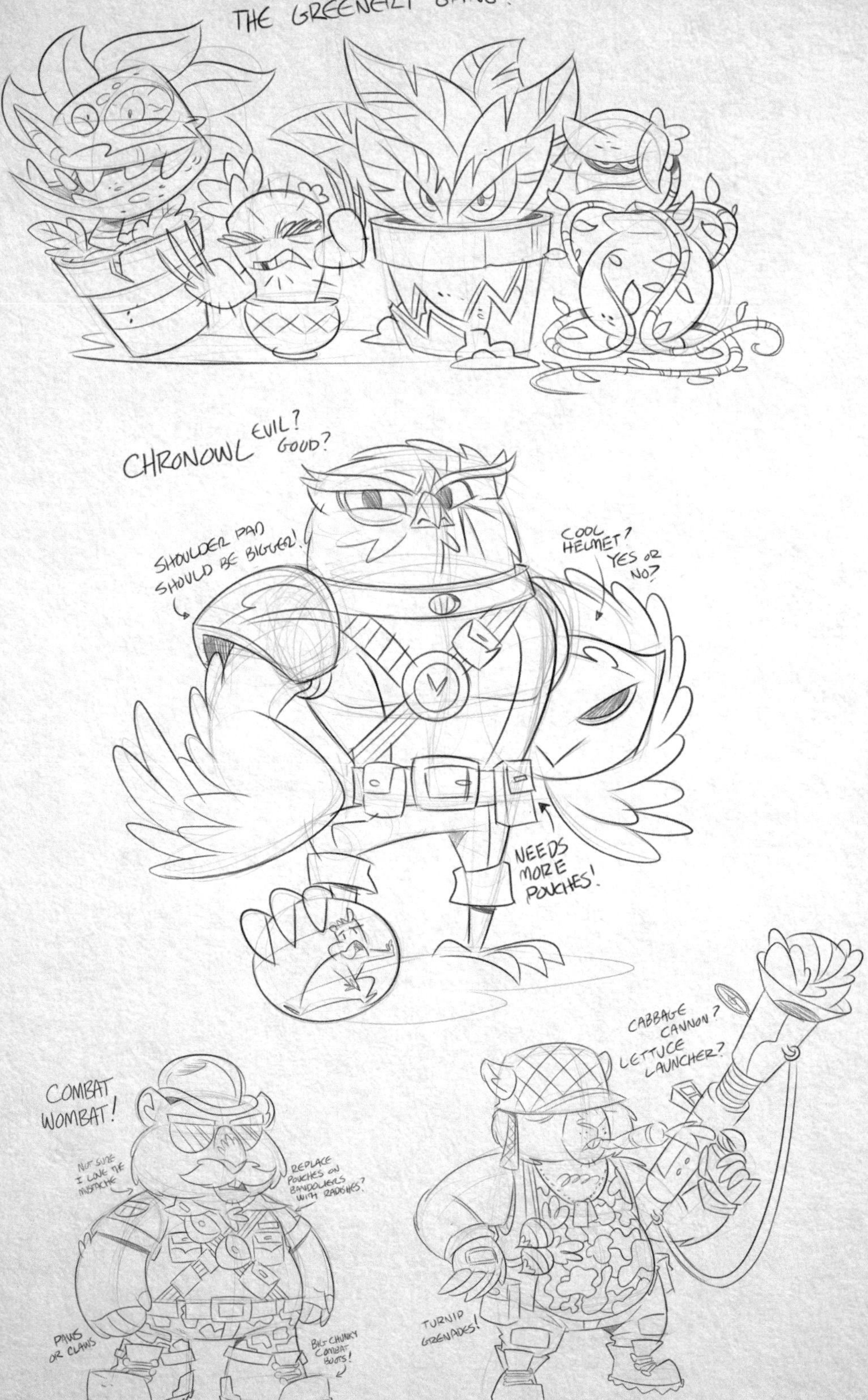

THE GREENERY GANG!
CHRONOWL
EVIL? GOOD?
SHOULDER PAD SHOULD BE BIGGER!
COOL HELMET? YES OR NO?
NEEDS MORE POUCHES!
COMBAT WOMBAT!
NOT SURE I LOVE THE MUSTACHE
REPLACE POUCHES ON BANDOLIERS WITH RADISHES?
PAWS OR CLAWS
BIG-CHUNKY COMBAT BOOTS!
CABBAGE CANNON? LETTUCE LAUNCHER?
TURNIP GRENADES!

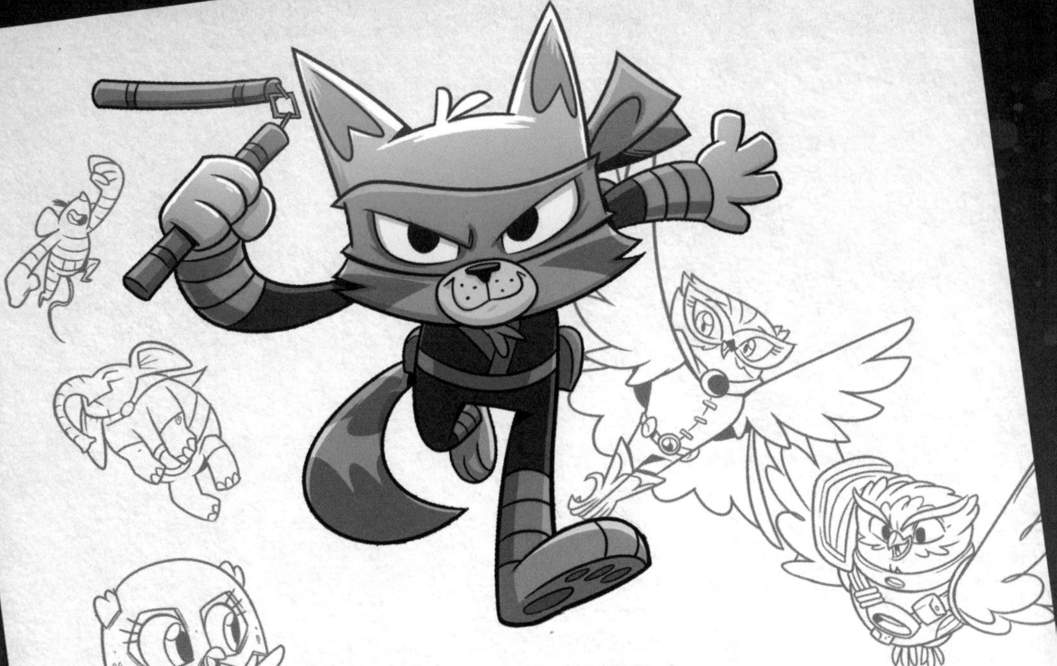

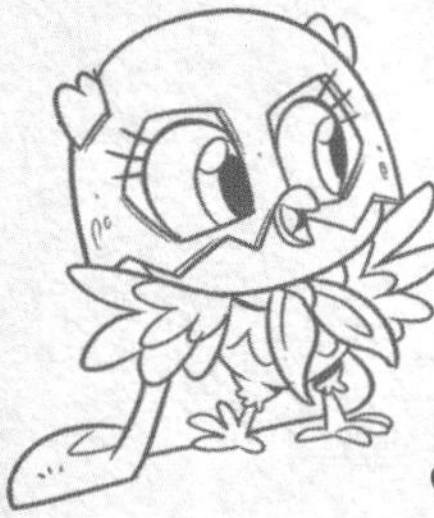

What Is Your Superhero Name?

Use the first letter of your first name and the last number of your birth year to learn your superhero name!

A - Marvelous
B - Captivating
C - Spectacular
D - Amazing
E - Brilliant
F - Extraordinary
G - Mind-Blowing
H - Incredible
I - Golden
J - Stupendous
K - Astonishing
L - Powerful
M - Glorious
N - Fabulous
O - Superb
P - Scarlet
Q - Sensational
R - Crafty
S - Royal
T - Astounding
U - Clever
V - Super
W - The Great
X - Giant
Y - Ultimate
Z - Nifty

1 - Genius
2 - Justice
3 - Blaster
4 - Prodigy
5 - Ninja
6 - Brain
7 - Might
8 - Protector
9 - Guardian
0 - Defender

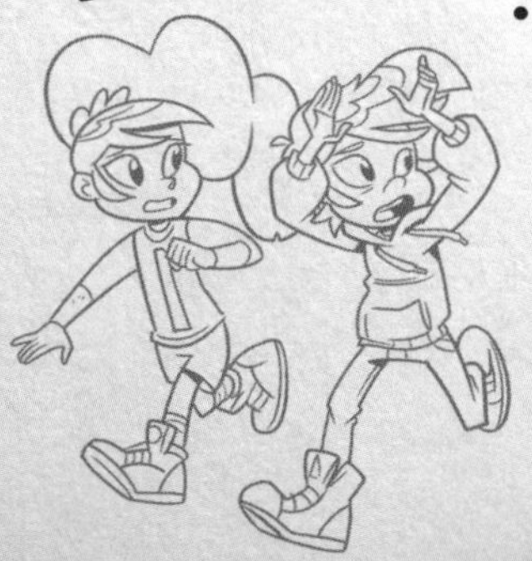

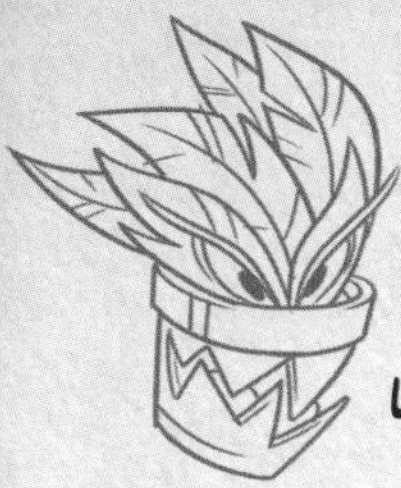

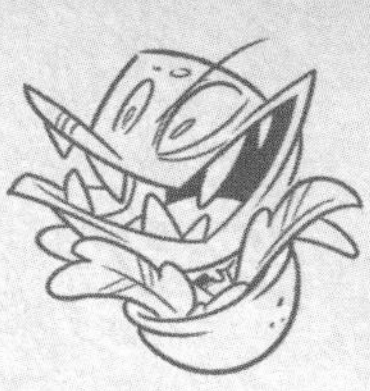

What Is Your Supervillain Name?

Use the month you were born and the day you were born to learn your supervillain name!

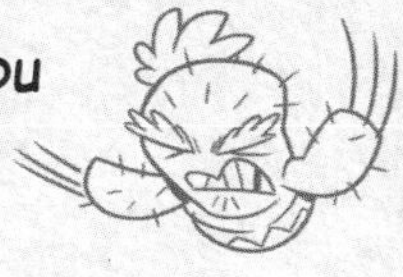

January – Rotten
February – Evil
March – Crusty
April – Diabolical
May – Hairy
June – Dastardly
July – Doomed
August – Vile
September – Cursed
October – Sinister
November – Foul
December – Malicious

1 – Sewer Rat
2 – Snot Spewer
3 – Denture Mouth
4 – Joker
5 – Twinkle Tamer
6 – Bubble Bottom
7 – Stinkbug
8 – Dumpster Diver
9 – Furball
10 – Garlic Nose
11 – Banana Peel
12 – Mastermind
13 – Garbage Gopher
14 – Jelly Belly
15 – Toothbrush
16 – Lobster Breath
17 – Doodler
18 – Tuna Tub
19 – Vermin
20 – Maniac
21 – Gunk Grabber
22 – Skunkmaster
23 – Mold Eater
24 – Opossum Poker
25 – Crustacean
26 – Milk Mustache
27 – Wubby Bubby
28 – Slimer
29 – Spinach Sniffer
30 – Fish
31 – Burp Thief

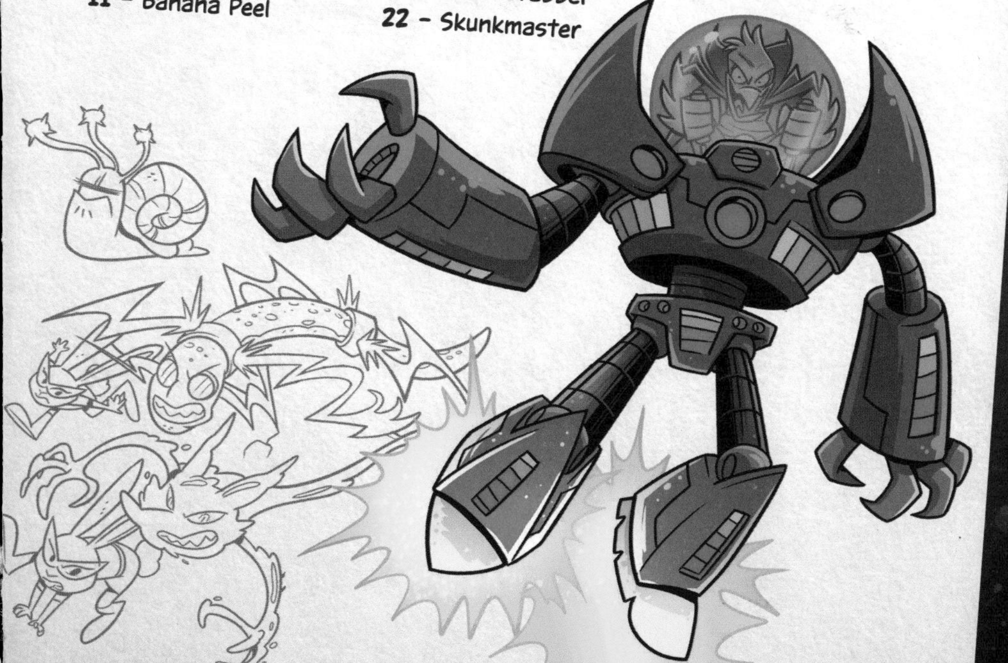

LOOK FOR THESE BOOKS FROM

epic!

AVAILABLE **NOW!**

TO READ MORE, VISIT
getepic.com